PLAYING WITH FIRE

PLAYING WITH FIRE

A New York Novel

F. R. HOTCHKISS

ISBN: 1539329038
ISBN 13: 9781539329039
Library of Congress Control Number: 2016916746
CreateSpace Independent Publishing Platform
North Charleston, South Carolina

TABLE OF CONTENTS

ONE

DECEPTIONS

At first glance, Benno Strong was almost a caricature of a New York advertising executive. A fit 55, he owned — and ran — a small but growing agency that provided a good living and was beginning to get important industry attention. He was tall and angular with brush-cut graying hair and a good physique that allowed him to run when he could squeeze it in. Fifteen miles a week was his goal.

When a late meeting kept him from commuting home, he would jog on the city's hard pavements, but what he loved most was a good run through the leafy roads in Connecticut where he lived. His wife wasn't a runner, and even if she had been, they would never have run together. Each reserved certain parts of their lives to themselves. Running was his alone. Strong was a happy man, and a happily married man. Success and independence hadn't come easily, so when they did come, he appreciated them all the more.

Like most people, he was not prepared for what came next.

◆ ◆ ◆

When the young woman breezed into the conference room, she struck Strong absolutely dumb.

Jet-black hair fell over a lipstick red dress cut just above the knee. He saw her legs outlined beneath the tight wool dress. Her tan calf muscles rippled over red patent leather heels as she stood with her legs close together. He couldn't look at her, and walked away when she tried to introduce herself. Her delicate perfume made him struggle to breathe. Good God, he was a happily married man – what in hell was he thinking?

Later, Strong sat in the back of the dark conference room, letting his henchmen negotiate a contract to bring her and her consulting team onboard for a month. As the owner of the advertising agency, he was a notorious tight-wad, but he would have paid a million dollars to be sure she was on board. After the meeting, in his office, when the door was closed and they were alone, he looked at her as if she were on fire.

◆ ◆ ◆

Natalia Tsukarova had heard about Strong. Madison Avenue was addicted to rumors. The rumor about Strong was that he was a creative but taciturn CEO of one of the best small agencies extant. Tomorrow she would lead a four-man team of computer graphics pros – at 33 she was the oldest by eight years – in a bid to win a month-long contract to bring Strong's creative department up to speed. Computer technology changed so fast that just keeping up with the latest software was a full-time job.

Sitting at her dressing table, she wondered what he was really like as she brushed her hair and looked herself in the eye in a silk robe and nothing else. There was an early thread of gray down the center of her hairline. She was trim, she was pleased to note. Swimming endless laps on the weekends kept her stomach flat. She sat up straight and turned slightly to admire her profile, then grimaced to see her teeth. Someday she would have the slight gap between her two front teeth closed. She had been saying that to herself ever since she first came to America sixteen years ago.

Friday, the morning of the meeting, Natalia put on a suit that flattered her long silhouette, shot some perfume beneath each ear, then paused and gave one final spritz to her chest. This should be fun, she thought. She wasn't nervous at all. Friday was her lucky day.

It was 10 AM when she walked in to Strong's small conference room and conversation stopped. A distin-guished-looking man with graying hair stared at her, then looked away and retreated to a distant corner. That must be Benno Strong, she thought. 'Quirky' is right! To hell with him. Let's take his bucks.

They made the pitch, made it damn well, complete with large-screen graphics and digitized sound. Strong's creative people tried not be impressed and failed. Natalia's team got the job. She knew they would. They were that good. That's food on the table, she thought. There had not always been food on the table.

In Strong's office, after the others drifted out, she was suddenly aware she was alone with him. She turned to say something jocular, but from his look, there was nothing to say. He stared at her as if he were on fire. She felt completely exposed, stark naked.

Natalia took off her glasses, set the briefcase down and walked straight up to him. Strong watched her as she approached until she stood a foot away. He had his hands in his pockets but looked as if he might spring at any moment, like a puma. She stared at him for a moment, then slapped him, hard. The impact made an awful sound, a crack. Natalia thought for sure the secretary would hear through the closed door and dial Security. The blow staggered him. He rocked back, and his eyes lost their focus. His hands came out his pockets and groped the air for balance. Natalia reached out to steady him. She hadn't meant to hurt him. She wanted to sober him.

"Are you all right?" she asked, horrified. She had never done anything like that in her life. He grabbed on to her arm in a daze to steady himself but almost fell.

Natalia left as fast as she could. The secretary watched her depart. That was how it began.

◆ ◆ ◆

Strong sat at his desk with his head still ringing like a bell. Mid-day sun poured in the floor-to-ceiling windows and cast stark shadows on the carpet. Across his desk was a scattering of small, framed photos — Strong and his wife on a beach in Bali, with his daughter climbing Mt. Whitney in California, with his wife in a hot tub somewhere.

Business was booming. He had built it from nothing and now it was beginning to win prizes. *Ad Age* had profiled him a year ago. For two days he had felt like a movie star. "Nice bit in the trades," strangers called out to him as he walked down Madison. He laughed it off, loving it. Billings topped $50 million. The agency had eighteen people packed onto the twenty-second floor of a good New York address.

He got up from his desk and headed for the door fifteen feet away, then strode down the long hall with turn-of-the-century posters his wife had selected on the walls. There was even an original Toulouse-Lautrec Bal Musette print. If the business died, he could always sell these and survive.

People were leaving for lunch, some of them young women. Strong liked working with women. He admired them, even loved them in an abstract, romantic way. For him they were bright spots to lighten the day, wonders to watch and admire from a distance.

There were a number of good-looking girls at the agency. Most of them didn't realize what they had, the beauty and power they carried inside. With a turn of the head or a look or just walking between desks, cutting one short and rolling around it with their hip, they could suck the air right out of him.

Strong knew women who understood their power, and who made very good use of the knowledge. Not that they slept around – they were smarter than that. They got men in the palm of their hand and kept them there, so these men had to concentrate to be able to hear what these smart women said. Strong had met powerful men who talked softly to ensure people listened carefully. It was the same thing.

Recently he had found himself nearly overwhelmed. He fell in love two or three times a week. It didn't mean anything. One time a new junior attorney had arrived for a meeting. She shook his hand firmly while her short blond hair slipped across her cheek.

"How do you do?" she had asked, giving her name.

Strong thought he might tumble face first into the cleavage at the top of her pinstriped, single-breasted suit. "Uh, fine, fine. Who are you? What was your name?" She repeated and he forgot it immediately.

He refused to look at her for the rest of the meeting, but noted that she crossed her legs exactly twelve times.

He switched law firms the next day. At $350 an hour, he could not afford to be thinking about sex.

Another time, at a family gathering – he suspected he should be truly ashamed of this – his wife's niece, all of 17 and bursting with energy, bounced up to him time after time with hors-d'oeuvres, drinks, anything to get close.

"Ben – I mean Mr. Strong – would you like one of these?" she asked, proffering a cheese puff.

Strong had a feeling she really meant her ample bust, but immediately dismissed the idea as fantasy.

"So, tell me all about advertising!" she said. The girl put down the puff tray and plopped down next to him on the chintz sofa, huge eyes wide with a look that asked him to jump right in. He pretended not to notice. His wife glanced at him from across the room. Signals were flying everywhere. Later he thanked his lucky stars he hadn't ended up alone with this underage girl because he realized what she had in mind and he wasn't 100 percent sure he would be able to resist.

Periodically in the country he got waylaid by a checker at the supermarket. Strong floated through with an occasional carton of milk or package of pasta. She always looked at him and said, "Oh, it's you again."

What the hell did I do? he wondered. At first he thought she was upset that he didn't have the right change, or he had too many groceries in the express lane, but eventually he realized he must have done something to her – touched her, affected her. He found that hard to believe.

Apparently she was waiting to see him again. He was the highlight of her day. He charged the moment; he was a fantasy in a long day of fruit, meat and vegetables. To cover it up she played it down: "Oh, it's you again."

Once he understood, he always went to her line. She seemed to realize he had caught on and they both laughed and asked real questions. The express lane became a bright spot in his week. She had kids. He had a wife. He liked her a lot and thought of her as a friend. She probably thought of him as something else, but would never act on it.

But this young consultant had literally taken his breath away. She was right to have slugged him. He respected her for that. He had never been unfaithful, and he wasn't going to start now.

◆ ◆ ◆

Riding home on the train, his cheek still throbbing, Strong spread out his paper, nodded to an acquaintance, and started reading. He couldn't get through a single sentence. Good God, what had come over him? Never before had he found a woman so beautiful that he had to walk away. He turned her over like a pebble in his mind, examining her this way and that as a small thrill began in his stomach and climbed into his throat.

Come on, he thought. You're happily married. Why are you dreaming about some girl who's twenty years

<u>younger – only a little older than Shelley</u>? Shelley had started talking to him again following three years of teen-age rejection. After two months in college she called and said in an angry voice, "Dad, you should have told me."

"Told you what?" he asked. There was a time when they could complete each other's sentences, but that time had passed.

"All the things you guys did for me." He and his wife were now "guys". On her own for the first time, Shelley was beginning to appreciate her parents. He laughed, and so did she.

"Well, I think I did but…"

"I know, I wasn't listening too well."

What in hell was he thinking? The young woman who had bowled him over was only a few years older than his own daughter! She wasn't perfect; there was a small gap between her two front teeth, but she was tall; she stood straight and fearless; she was proud of her small chest; she had long, long legs; she looked right at him; she wasn't afraid of anything, he was sure; her hair was like pitch. He shook his head violently and rubbed his eyes.

This is ridiculous, he said to himself. Stop it! Strong folded the paper, got off the train at his stop and, wrapped against the cold, kissed his wife as he climbed in the waiting car. He mumbled an excuse about his face, which made her take a second look. When they arrived home they shared a laugh or two and then he grabbed her from behind and she said, "Oh…" He pulled her into the bedroom and made love to her like he hadn't made love in ten years. They were both breathless.

"Ben, I don't know what you did in the city today, but I hope you do it again. Maybe you should run into a door more often," she said touching his face, and they laughed.

Thank God, Strong said to himself later, when he realized he hadn't so much as thought of the girl for one second the rest of the night. In the morning he jogged six miles, twice his normal distance.

◆ ◆ ◆

When the graphics training began on Monday, Strong was there to greet everyone on the new team, especially the girl in her chic gray suit with blue pearls and her pitch-black hair. Open laptops covered the conference table. Each of his people had a trainer beside them, ready to go.

"Hey, everyone, happy Monday!" he said too loudly to the assembled crowd.

"Oh no, he's here," someone said in the back of the room.

"I heard that!" Strong said, and they all laughed.

He was glad she was there with her team. He had no ulterior motives. They were going to make a difference in the ads he produced and the speed they could get them out, Strong was sure. He looked at them all and said,

"Start of a big day," and clapped his hands as if it were cold. He could tell they were surprised the boss was there, but they were also pleased. The mood was electric, and it was only Monday.

Strong had wondered if he would get short of breath when she walked in, but he didn't. Thank God – he was cured. An illusion, a deception, a silly whim had made him act stupidly. Was it only last Friday? He had been such a fool. He was so embarrassed. How do I handle this? He thought. What do I say?

He wanted to let her know his absurd infatuation was past, forgotten and gone forever. At the first opportunity, he walked up and said, "Hi! Look, I want to apologize. I don't know what came over me. I'm so embarrassed. Please forgive me."

"Thank you. But you barely know my name. And I am not dead sure of yours," she replied. They had never introduced themselves in so many words.

"Oh. I'm Benno Strong."

"And I am Natalia Tsukarova."

"Ah." He nodded as if he understood.

"It's Russian. You won't be required to spell it."

He laughed. "Yes, well I hope you are OK," Strong said. "I hope I haven't … caused you any pain." He wanted to run out of the room.

Natalia wasn't sure what she was hearing. She had thought about him over weekend without knowing what to think. She had hit him full force in the face, and here he was talking about her pain. What was she supposed to make of a man who looked at her as if he saw right down to the soles of her feet? He had made her shiver. Then she had acted completely irrationally and slapped him. Stay away from this guy, she had decided.

Natalia foresaw either an inept come-on or complete denial. She had half expected to get fired. When Strong apologized, she found herself replying, "Thank you for saying that. It was exactly what I was thinking. I should also apologize."

"No, no. I'm completely to blame." He clapped his hands together again. People turned to look. "Now that we've got that behind us, if there is any way I can help you here, you must let me know."

"I will. Thank you. I had better be getting started. Your face…?"

"Does it still show? You pack a hell of a punch, you know." He chuckled. "I told everyone a beautiful girl hit me. They all laughed – they didn't believe me. Actually, that's the only thing that really hurt." She laughed despite herself.

"Listen, watch out for these guys," he said. "They might try to trip you up sometimes. I'd love you to impress them."

"I will do my best," she promised, and they shook hands formally.

Back in his corner office, Strong shut the door. Well, that's that, he thought. He was sweating and wished he still smoked.

At the end of the day, he found an excuse to drift down the hall to the reception desk to see her leave. It was after six o'clock. The place was abandoned. She came down the hallway looking frazzled and not particularly glad to see him. The gray strand of hair had come unraveled and hung over her forehead.

"Well, how'd it go?" he asked.

"Great." she said. "They are arrogant as hell, but they're listening. It is about as much as you can ask the first day out."

"You mean we're going to get our money's worth for all this..." he left it hanging in the air.

"Crap," she finished for him. She seemed a little miffed. "Good night." She turned and was gone.

Strong began a slow burn. God was she touchy! Well, let her finish her job and get out of here. That was fine by him. To hell with her, he thought.

On the train that night, he read the paper all the way home without a problem.

◆ ◆ ◆

As Natalia rode the bus to her apartment in the Village, she leaned her head against the cold window and drifted in and out of consciousness. She thought she had situation in hand but she was so startled by his concern when she had walked in that she dropped pencils and papers the rest of the day.

And then at the end, when he was obviously waiting to see her in the lobby, he had made that inane remark about training, and she had said something bitchy. Why in the world did she do that? You didn't talk to a client like that. He got a hurt look in his eyes and she had left. Oh, to hell with this whole thing! Just finish the job and get out of there. Some situations were hopeless.

TWO

Business as Usual

Benno Strong was a showman, an actor, a performer more than a businessman. He would have made a good attorney or college professor. His mother had given him his unusual name over his father's objections, and it fit. She was second-generation Italian, and a former actress to boot. Strong's creative side came from her, he was sure. It was the part of him he liked best. His peers thought of him as a clever advertiser, a term he didn't particularly like because he had been a whole lot of things a whole lot longer – teen creep, hippie, soldier, then journalist and now businessman.

Strong knew a few people who were great business-men. They never sold anything. On the contrary, they presented an opportunity so appealing that clients took it for steak and dug right in. Strong wasn't that clever, but he was good at seeing what was already in front of clients' faces, seeing what they had forgotten, and helping them believe in their products again. He could walk into a roomful of stuffed shirts, begin talking quietly, and slowly light the fire under these florid-faced men who were getting paid more money than even they could believe, easing them slowly forward in their seats as he showed how to present their product, how to get excited about it, how to make others think it was special, and how it *was* special, although they had probably forgotten. There was always something unique about a product or service. Strong's job was to find that essence, and to revive the dream in its creators. Once he made them excited again, it was only a matter of agreeing on the price and signing the contract.

One client, a neophyte cell phone company, had asked him to boost its infinitesimal sales with a campaign focusing on newspapers. Newspaper advertising was all they could afford.

He went home and pondered. He still smoked at the time, and lit a cigarette with a glass of wine after dinner, nestled in a comfortable leather club chair in the den. What was unique about cell phones? What was the real message here? Except for business, Strong hated cell phones. He thought of them as an intrusion into private time, but at the same time he loved the idea of being able to talk spontaneously to anyone, anywhere, anytime, at the drop of a hat. That thrilled him. This was in the early '90s when cell phones were rare. Out of nowhere, he said, "Hah!" and actually snapped his fingers. Then he laughed.

At their next meeting, held at the company's "head-quarters" around two card tables jammed together surrounded by folding plastic chairs, he told his clients, "It's not a phone you're selling. It's convenience." They all looked confused – even the president, who couldn't have been more than 32.

"Shoot a commercial of people in-line skating with a phone," he said, "Or in an elevator with a phone, on the toilet with a phone, disco dancing with a phone, doing anything with a phone, and put it on MTV and Black Entertainment Television." Those were relatively inexpensive outlets, he explained.

They looked shocked, then one by one began to laugh. Eventually they stood up and applauded.

Sales multiplied by a factor of ten. The phone folks gave him a twenty percent bonus at year's end and an option on 10,000 shares in the company, just so he wouldn't take on any other cell phone accounts.

Once, over a second martini, it occurred to Strong he was giving his clients faith in what they did, faith in what they had – both in themselves and their future. That's why people paid him so much. I am a priest of the new godless order, he thought blurredly. In the morning he realized he had been drunk.

◆ ◆ ◆

Three weeks went by and Strong had almost forgotten the young woman with the strange name – Suka-something. Natalia, he could remember. They hadn't even bumped into each other – not that the agency was that big. The first week he had drifted out of his office a few times in the off chance he might see her, but he never did. After a while, he was glad. She was like a bruise – something that hurt but he still wanted to touch or worry, like a loose tooth. She was best left alone and forgotten.

Strong's office manager came in to give the final report on the graphics seminars. He was gay as the day was long, and he didn't give the tiniest damn who knew it. That's why I hired this guy, Strong remembered. He's got balls! The irony made him laugh.

"So, how was it?" Strong asked.

"I know you hate this training stuff, you think everyone should learn on their own time after work, come in here on weekends, or maybe stay until midnight five days a week – you know, just get it, but that's not the way it works. You pay people to learn these days." It wasn't the first time he had accused Strong of being tight-fisted.

"So, was it worth it?"

"I learned a lot, I can tell you that. That girl Natalia Whatever was particularly good. You got your money's worth, and a whole lot more."

Strong didn't say anything for a bit. "Are you putting me on? Was she that good?"

"Just watch the production for the next six months, and you tell me," his manager said.

Well, that's a pretty good recommendation, Strong thought. "I guess we need to have a party to say, 'Thanks.'" The man nodded. Strong delighted in throwing good parties, which were popular for their excellent wines.

◆ ◆ ◆

They held the party at the previous year's "in" spot. The place looked like the owners had run out of money before it was finished, with exposed heating ducts and unfinished walls. Strong would never have chosen the place on his own, but everyone at the agency had insisted.

Natalia came in a dark green dress, subtle and revealing at the same time, with its long sleeves and low back. He didn't speak to her until halfway through dinner when he summoned up the courage and went over to her table, carrying his wine glass with him. "Thank you," he said pure and simple, by means of congratulations.

She didn't look at him for a moment, staring straight ahead over her plate, then turned on him full in the face. "You're welcome. I was wondering if you were avoiding me."

"I apologize. I've been busy." He paused, and started all over again. "Why is it with you I always seem to be on the defensive? The last time it was for a left hook." The guy sitting next to her stopped his fork in mid-air.

"Sit down," Natalia ordered, and he did. "You are a rather difficult person to talk to."

The irritation in her voice pleased him for some reason. He took a sip of wine. "Do you always flatter the clientele like this, or is this a new way of doing things? You must have gone to the New York School For Waiters."

The guy with the fork next to her laughed out loud. She didn't respond.

This is going nowhere, he thought and started to get up.

She put a hand on his wrist. "Wait. Wait. I am sorry. I do not know why I said that. I am being such a bitch, what is wrong with me? It is just that I was hoping you would come to some of the sessions, see us in action, see what we could do. We are really pretty good, you know."

He noticed she seldom used contractions. "I never doubted it. You don't have to worry, you guys all get an A-plus."

"Guys" seemed a completely inappropriate term for her. For the first time since she had marched out of his office, he dared to look directly into her eyes. He was surprised to see they were dark brown. How could he have missed that? She had tinted her eyelids with a subtle shade of green, complementing her dress. Her lipstick was a very dark red color. She may have been small-breasted but there was definitely something there, and she seemed pleased to show it. Strong loved that. He wanted to put his fingers to her lips to see how soft they were. He felt awkward, like a teenager on a first date. Why couldn't he just be pleasant and not be an idiot with this woman?

He stumbled on. "Look, I have a proposition."

Her immediate neighbor choked on his wine and groped for his napkin to clean up. She took a breath and opened her lips to say something. He put his hand up to stop her expected riposte to the word "proposition".

"I am bound and determined to stop acting like a jerk when I speak to you," he blurted out, "and I'm not having much success. Would you mind joining me at the bar while I see if a little liquid refreshment might help?"

She looked at him without a word.

"Please. I'm really trying here."

She smiled, folded her napkin on the table and got up. "It is the middle of dinner, you know."

He carefully took her arm and steered her towards the bar. "My wife refuses to come to these things. She thinks they are a complete bore, and as far as the people at my table tonight are concerned, she's right. Think of this as a mission of mercy." She was wearing the same rich perfume, he noticed.

Two hours later, they were still at the bar. The party had long since broken up. People had sought him out to say good-bye. He thanked them perfunctorily, and they departed.

Strong enjoyed himself immensely, and he wasn't even high. Natalia had come down off her pedestal and laughed without reservation. She was damn quick and bright, that was for sure. She had sparkle and style; he couldn't imagine her ever eating something so humble as a hamburger. "When was the last time you ate at McDonald's?" he asked impulsively.

"God, I am not that hungry, even though we missed dinner," she said.

"No, no, that's not what I meant," he said. "Really – the last time?"

She looked at him quizzically. "About four years ago. Why?"

"Tell you some other time." He thought, This is no fast-food woman. Whoever ends up with her is going to have to really pay the bill.

Natalia Tsukarova sat perched on a stool with her legs crossed, elbows on the zinc bar, and told him about herself. She was Soviet Georgian – she spelled out her last name carefully and he promised never to forget, then promptly did. She had stayed in Russia until she was 17, when she emigrated, always dreaming of the United States but never really thinking it was possible until the Soviet Union imploded and people started scrambling for the borders. She had lived in Tbilisi, then the Crimea for high school. She knew caviar inside and out; she had a taste for vodka, but was still learning about wine. Americans thought Russian wine was always sweet. It wasn't. She was sipping a martini with five olives on the side. Strong felt like he was in a movie.

"What was Russia like?" he wanted to know.

Her father had been an official, high-placed he guessed but she didn't say. Her mother was from the Caucasus, dark and passionate, and he imagined Natalia might be the same. He thought he could occasionally see the outline of a nipple beneath the material of her dress, but he tried not to look. She spoke with almost no accent at all.

"I had heard some things about you before I came," she said, not looking at him.

"Uh-oh, this sounds bad," he replied, hoping it wasn't.

"I heard you were different. Not a typical business type. They didn't tell me any specifics. When I met you, I thought you were a jerk. Before the left hook."

That made him laugh. "So you thought I was a jerk right off the bat. What did I do to deserve that?"

"Plenty. I said 'hello' and you did not say anything, even when I put out my hand."

"I was looking at you, and then … I couldn't look at you any more, so I didn't." He didn't want to get into this, and looked down at his glass.

"Oh," she said and turned. "You are not looking at me now."

"Not yet." He took a big sip. "Now I am," he said with a forced smile.

"How brave."

Strong decided it was safer to say nothing at all, so he didn't.

"And you – who are you?" she asked.

To his surprise, he plunged right in. Normally it was a question he avoided. "Well, I'm certainly not who you think I am."

"Which is what?"

"Mr. American Adman with the big house in the country and the lovely family and the European car and the…" he stopped when he realized he had been describing himself a little too close to the bone. She waited for him to recover.

"Actually, I am all that, but it isn't really … isn't really <u>who</u> I am."

She looked at him with a small smile and waited.

And then he began telling her things that he hadn't told anyone in a very long time. He had always been an observer who watched everything and everyone around him, as if recording it all for some future tale.

He had seen people killed. One bright sunny day in a helicopter in Southeast Asia he saw the pilot flip down his gun sight and take aim. There were people in the rice paddies below, in the wrong place on a map. They kept working and didn't look up when the bullets splashed around them, and then tore home. A woman and a man fell face first in the mud. Strong wanted to shriek. The sight was too much even for the gun crew. One of them said, "Let's get the fuck out of here," and they did. He had even killed people. In war, when the other side shot, you didn't call "Time out!" and have a chat.

When he finished the story, he realized he had seen it all over again. He took a breath. She was listening. He kept on.

Before that, he had lived in Europe. He wasn't comfortable in his own country, as affected as that might sound. In Paris he felt alive. He was a student, free to do anything – or not do a damn thing. For quite a while he didn't do much but roam the streets and galleries. One day he woke up to find he was hungry to learn in a way he had never been, and he stayed hungry for six glorious months. When he returned to earth, he realized that the French, though wonders at wine and cheese, were just as venal, frugal, and selfish as everyone else, and maybe a bit more. He came home.

"But when I was there, there was a man. He looked like a banker. I was in an elevator. He was talking intensely to someone and suddenly he burst out crying, tears just pouring down his cheeks." She listened intently.

"He didn't cover his face with his hands, like we would here. He just kept talking in this impassioned way, the tears flowing. He reminded me of that Cartier-Bresson photograph of the fall of Paris to the Germans, a man weeping openly at the side of the road to see his nation crumble.

"No one in the elevator seemed shocked or embarrassed. I was struck by it. It was so forthright and honest. He wasn't ashamed of his feelings. No one was ashamed for him. I admired that. I thought, 'That's the way I would like it to be.' It's not the way we Americans are. Is this making sense?"

"I think so, although I wouldn't expect it from a businessman. Maybe an artist. Are you really like that?" She squinted at him as if to see him better.

"You tell me."

"OK, I will, someday. You don't sound like an American. You sound like a Russian."

He laughed. "A long time ago, a girlfriend told me I had a Jewish soul. For a *goy*, that was a great compliment. Where I grew up, I didn't even know any Democrats much less Jews till I went away to college."

He rambled on, talked about meeting his wife, their happy years together, their daughter Shelley. He wanted Natalia to know about his family, but did not dwell on it. He had an overwhelming desire to teach her what he knew. He was sure she would understand everything the first time. He listened to himself and realized he sounded like a dreamer, which he was, although few people knew it. He had forgotten it himself. He usually kept a pretty tight lip. He felt exhilarated, alive, refreshed. He felt wonderful. When she slipped off the stool to leave, he stood primly and offered his hand. She took it.

"This was a most enjoyable evening for me," he said somewhat awkwardly. He was a little drunk, but he meant it.

She held onto his hand until she said, "For me, also," then turned and left.

Strong heard the clack of her heels and watched the shape of her dress as she walked away. Would she turn to wave goodbye? She was a beautiful woman. He wasn't sure she knew it.

She turned the corner without looking back, and was gone.

◆ ◆ ◆

That night on the last train to the country, he looked out the window at the blur of wet trees and warehouse lights and thought, That was great. He had forgotten what it was like to have a long, absorbing conversation with someone, and it filled a forgotten need. He and his wife sometimes talked like that, but not too often any more. Besides, she knew everything about him already. There were no secrets.

He no longer felt sensual about this girl, he was pleased to note as he listened to the clack of the wheels on the tracks. No tug of the heart pulled him down. No, on the contrary, he felt free. He didn't want passion. He was married, happily married.

Strong had to admit that when he first met her, there was an incredible pull of passion, a deep, dark, compelling attraction that was beyond reason. It had overwhelmed him like a storm. He watched the rain pour down through the passing lights as the train pierced the night.

She had seemed so striking, so uniquely beautiful. My God, how he had stared at her! He didn't blame her one bit for slapping him full in the face. In fact, he was thankful. The blow had brought him around. Now he and Natalia were beyond that. They were two people beginning a friendship. It felt good to have a new friend. He had so few, less than the fingers on one hand. A lot less. Maybe a thumb.

The wail of the whistle reminded him of distant memories, of time passing, of loneliness.

Opening up was refreshing. No, more than that. It was rejuvenating. That is the right word, he said to his reflection in the rain-streaked window. The prospect of a friend like Natalia was exciting. Perhaps he would get close to the edge of friendship, but he would be certain not to go over it. The two of them would have long conversations at lunch about history and art and social change, things that would seem sophomoric with anyone else. He recalled such lunches in Paris, fraught with earnestness and volume and verve.

He laughed out loud in the nearly empty train.

He had an idea how she would think, with her European education seasoned by current feminist predilections. He looked forward to the discussions. There would be an age difference, as well as a gender battle.

As for passion, he was cured. He could feel it. The poison was out of his system.

"Thank God for that," he said out loud. A woman across the aisle opened one eye, then closed it and went back to sleep.

◆ ◆ ◆

Three weeks later, Natalia called. Strong sat at his desk going over the graphics on the cell phone account, which had burgeoned to five million dollars. His secretary buzzed him that she was calling, and he picked up the phone without looking at it. "Hello?"

"Do you accept professional invitations from former business associates?" she asked.

"Is this the lady with the great right cross?"

She burst out laughing. "Left hook. I'm left-handed, remember? Will you ever forget that?"

"I hope not. How could I have made that mistake?" he replied.

She went on. "But I'm being serious now, professional, the way I ought to be. Can you speak at a conference my company is holding? You could talk about anything you wanted, within reason."

He heard the smile in her voice. This woman knows how to be enticing.

"How about winning new business – how to wow them in the boardroom?" he posed.

"I love it! I bet you'll pack the house. You know, almost everyone I know is terrified of that kind of thing. Will you really do it?"

"Hey, you asked me, I said I would, what more is there to say?"

"Ooh, I could just kiss you for that." She resumed her professional tone. "It's at the Plaza," she said, and filled in the details.

Two weeks, he thought. Well, that would give him enough time to make sure he didn't make an ass out of himself. He hung up the phone and went back to work.

Later in the day Strong found himself thinking of her in a paternal way. He was impressed with her maturity, her confidence, her womanliness. For some reason he felt proud of her.

THREE

WOMEN

Women were so different. He had all but forgotten. On the street he began noticing how remarkable they were. He was thrilled by the way they cocked a foot or tilted their heads in a particularly feminine way as they looked in a shop window or waited for an elevator. Strong felt like a teenager all over again, in unabashed awe of the female of the species. Their bodies didn't amaze him, although those could certainly get his attention. What fascinated him was their manner.

Occasionally a woman would catch him looking at her out of the corner of her eye and she would turn on him, ready for battle, but then she looked away and smiled, realizing he was an innocent admirer. These women made him laugh at his own gawkishness.

He fell in love ten times that week. Once, outside Saks, he stopped dead in his tracks when he caught sight of a mid-thirties blonde perusing the windows in snug jeans, an ankle-length mink coat and high heels. Another time, near Cooper Union, a buxom redheaded co-ed with just a shade of eye shadow and a backpack walked by and he paused to catch his breath.

On the train home an Asian in a short skirt, who was reading the *Journal* with her legs up on the opposing seat, had looked at him square in the face with an expression that said, "You got a problem, mister?"

Strong opened his paper and began reading furiously. If he could have, he would have fled to the next car.

He was sure other men understood women much better than he, and dealt with them much better. For those men, relationships were easy. For him, they were difficult indeed. He was convinced those men would not be flustered by a woman's glance. Why am I? he asked himself.

◆ ◆ ◆

Two weeks passed. The day before his scheduled talk on success in the boardroom, Natalia called to remind him. Strong didn't like being checked up on.

"Hey, it's me, Natalia" she said when he picked up the phone and said, "Yeah?"

"Yeah?" he repeated, focused on the layouts spread over his desk.

"Remember tomorrow?"

"Yeah." Of course he remembered. What is wrong with this woman? He picked up a red marker and made a slash through one of the proposed ads, killing it.

"OK. 'Bye."

"Fine. 'Bye."

She hung up, bang.

◆ ◆ ◆

His talk was good. He held it in the hotel boardroom to help his young audience get used to an intimidating setting. Strong wanted them to think of the boardroom as a façade, like a movie set.

Looking at the assembled group, he liked what he saw. They were all budding professionals new to the game – young, eager, some minorities, buttoned down and dressed up, bright people with fire in their eyes.

"It's their game," he said as he stood before them and motioned to the paneled walnut and the imaginary executives that usually held sway there. "They think they hold all the cards here." Recessed overhead spots threw shafts of light on original art on the walls, and illuminated the inch-deep carpeting.

"That's why you're invited to meet in a room like this – to be overwhelmed. Then you're putty. But if people rely on their surroundings to make them strong," he continued, one finger raised, "it means they are weak, vulnerable.

"Dark suits, gray hair and impassive faces are meant to intimidate. That's their game. So don't be intimidated." He watched them exchange looks and nods, and it suddenly occurred to him that he might look a lot like the men he was describing.

"By the way, they're not bad people. As a matter of fact, a lot of them are just like you – scared. You may think they are bastards who hate women in the boardroom," he said, nodding to a young blonde who smiled at everything he said, "but that's not it. Women throw them off; they don't play by the same rules. That disorients these guys, undercuts their power. That's why there aren't a whole hell of a lot of women up there on the fortieth floor." He paced back and forth at the end of the long waxed table that glistened as if someone had just thrown water over it.

Strong stopped. "'Course I think there may be another reason as well. Most women, once they see the corporate folderol, avoid it like the plague. They move on to better things."

To his delight there were some chuckles of agreement among the youngish crowd, particularly the females. He was hitting home.

He leaned forward with both hands on the table. "Go into a meeting having done your homework. Be certain that you have a good idea.

"Let the idea speak for itself. If the people you are pitching are too stupid to 'get' it, you don't want them for a client anyway. If they get the message, you've just paid for lunch. Speaking of which," he said with a glance at his watch, "why don't we go get some?"

They all laughed. A few clapped.

Natalia stood in the back of the room, leaning against the wall. She wore a deep blue suit with a bright Frank Lloyd Wright scarf of dark red and yellow. While he talked, he never looked at her directly, but he never stopped seeing her, either. He remembered a basketball game in junior high school. He was crazy about one of the cheerleaders. He had never spoken to her, but he played each point for her, and the sight of her out of the corner of his eye spurred him on. He would have died for her.

He looked around at the faces at the table. "One final thing. Have fun. If you don't, business isn't worth it," he said in closing. They applauded and began to make their way to the door. He grinned like a proud parent.

A young Pakistani girl with doe eyes slithered up to ask a question. "Mr. Strong, do you suppose ..."

Strong turned to listen and caught a flash of bright scarf as Natalia cut the girl right off. "He has a lunch meeting. Why don't you come to the afternoon session?" The hostility in her voice made him smile.

As they moved out of the room Strong whispered, "I didn't know we were going for lunch."

"Well, now you know," she said simply and took him by the arm to the elevator, then downstairs and outside to a small French place down the street with waiters in white aprons from waist to floor. He let himself be guided along. This was fun. She was in charge.

"How have you been?" he asked once they were seated at a table with a white linen tablecloth and bentwood and cane chairs.

"I have missed you," she said frankly.

Strong sat up straight in his chair. "You missed me?" he asked. How could a young woman like her miss me? I must be her father's age, he thought briefly, and then stopped thinking about it. He didn't want to think of her having a father.

"I missed talking like we did."

"Now that you mention it, so did I," he said jocularly. "Actually, I was looking forward to seeing you again. There's a lot I would like to tell you."

"I will be a willing student and an ardent listener, but first we eat," she said.

"*Da*," he said in a deep voice, trying to sound Russian.

◆ ◆ ◆

After lunch they went for a walk. Strong buried his hands in his pockets. Natalia held onto his arm. Her scarf blew, along with wisps of her hair. He was completely at ease. The sun warmed his face in the blowing wind. Once he stepped in front of her to shield her from a particularly strong gust. He wanted to protect her. She seemed vulnerable to him, despite her strength.

There was something primordial about sheltering her, some rite that went far back beyond memory and history and was important, forceful, relevant.

As he stood in front of her and hid her from the wind and blowing dust, she slowly touched her forehead to the middle of his back. That stood him up straight like a fastball high and inside.

The light changed. They didn't move. People flowed around them. He turned around.

"We should go back," she finally said, looking up. The afternoon session would start in a few minutes, although he wasn't on the schedule.

"Yeah. Shit. Damn," he said.

"Me, too," she replied. "All three."

He took her arm – she gave it willingly – and they crossed the street. In the lobby he looked directly in her face without saying a word. She held his gaze. He slowly leaned forward and touched her forehead with his lips. She shut her eyes.

"Have a good afternoon," he said.

"I will. Will you call me?", she asked, looking at him again.

"You think I could help it?"

"Here. Home," she wrote on the back of a card. "I want to see you ... some more."

"Me, too." He could barely get the words out.

She turned and walked away, head down. When she got to the elevator, she turned and looked at him without breaking her gaze. The elevator came and went.

Strong bolted out into the Manhattan street sunlight. Oh, boy. Got to keep this under control, he thought as he hurried unseeing down the afternoon street, bumping into people. I can do that. His forehead was damp. The noise of the traffic, the occasional honk, brought him around. I'll be OK. Besides, how often do you meet someone who stirs the soul? He almost laughed out loud, that sounded so adolescent, even to a romantic like him.

FOUR

DECEPTION

Strong resisted calling as long as he could – four days. Toward the end, he thought he might explode, as if he were holding his breath and running out of air. He kept recalling how Natalia returned his looks steadily, without fear. Walking down the street, the thought of her would buffet him, mid-step. She was all there. In his mind he would turn away, as he had done several times over that lunch, afraid to look her full in the face for fear he would fall in. At home he moved around as if underwater.

When he finally called, Natalia was furious he had kept her waiting so long, and overjoyed that he had called at all. He was all she had been thinking about. One thing would never change, no matter how modern she tried to be: For her, it was the man who had to call. He had to take the first step. She might be liberated, but she was damned if she was ever going to violate that little rule. She also liked to have doors opened for her. To hell with Gloria Steinem.

When the phone rang in her compact apartment on the fourth day of ache and pain, she stared at it for three rings, afraid to answer. What if it wasn't him?

"It's me," he said.

She cocked one foot behind her and twirled slightly on the other. "How nice of you to call." There were many messages in that simple phrase – fury, passion, and doubt among them – and she hoped that he caught them all.

She heard him take a breath. "Look, I have been trying <u>not</u> to call you for the last – I don't know, what was it, a year since I saw you – and I couldn't do it. Goddamnit, I tried. Don't give me a lot of crap for calling. If you don't want to talk, just hang the hell up!"

The force of his confession melted her completely. She said, "I'm sorry. No, I am so glad you called. I was afraid you weren't going to."

It was the honest truth, something that didn't always come easily for her. Why did he do this to her? Why did she tell him that? She could feel tears welling up and tried hard to blink them away.

She had learned early on it was dangerous to be too open with men, and for them to be too open with her. Sometimes it took the magic out of things. When she was ten, she had been playing with her cousin and she wanted to see him – all of him. It was as simple as that. She was curious. She had seen her father naked countless times, so there was no suspense there, but her cousin was a mystery she wanted to solve. She goaded and chided him until he awkwardly dropped his pants. She was fascinated. It was so small, so silly looking, so innocent. What was the big deal? When he demanded reciprocity, she laughed in his face and refused to expose herself, not that she really cared. She just wasn't going to do it.

All this flashed through her mind as she held onto the phone. She heard Strong breathe and waited for him to say something. She loved the sound of his voice, his breathing.

"How have you been?" he finally asked, apparently trying to put things back on an even keel.

"Good. Actually, I've been walking all over the city trying to sort this out." She fiddled with the phone cord, twisting it around one finger.

"What do you mean by 'this'?" he asked.

"You know damn well what I mean."

"Yes, I guess I do," he said.

She had taken the subway to the South Street Seaport and hiked practically without halt all the way to the Seventies, thinking about him. It had been a beautiful day in the middle of the week. She had called in "sick", which everyone knew she wasn't. She did that periodically. It was accepted. She wore jeans and a short gray rabbit jacket. Her outfit showed off her butt and long legs and hinted at her bust. A cool breeze blew in her face. She ate a Polish sausage with steamed onions and mustard and a

Coke halfway along her journey of looking in antique store windows, browsing used book stores, pondering people as they marched toward her down the eastside streets.

All the while, in the back of her mind, at the tip of her heart, Strong was there, nibbling away, try as she might to expel him. For the first time, she realized she was on a slippery slope, sliding down it faster and faster. Despite herself, she couldn't wait to get to the bottom. She almost forgot the phone in her hand.

There was solidity to him. He had strength, like a boulder in white water. Most men she had known were too young to know who they truly were, but not this guy. Not that she didn't have older male friends. Like most attractive young women, she had admirers who pretended their feelings were platonic – former professors with whom she played tennis, a business associate who was a native New Yorker and took her to unusual, out-of-the-way places. Once they had eaten in an Italian restaurant in a basement of what seemed to be someone's apartment in the Village, with the kitchen in the middle and people at tiny tables in the back "garden" and the front living room. The waiters sang Puccini. From then on, she loved New York.

She had been lost in her thoughts. "I'm listening," he prompted.

"Oh. Well, I met this guy – this older man who is completely tied up – who is, I don't know, *fascinating* to me for a lot of reasons, and the last thing I want to do is get involved, if you know what I mean."

That got a reaction. "Right. Well, first things first. Could we take this 'older man' thing and throw it right the hell out the window? It doesn't mean a damn thing to me," he said. "I'm not arthritic, you know. No aluminum walkers in sight."

"Don't be so sensitive. Age doesn't mean anything to me, either. How old are you?"

"None of your business."

She let out a hoot. "Oh come on, get it out, get over it. It's not important. Just tell me. Bet you're not as old as my grandfather."

"Hey, screw you."

She pondered the thought for a long moment. "How old?"

He growled. "I'm forty-nine – and I have been for some time now."

She burst out laughing. She could hear the humor in his voice. "You really are something. OK, forget it. Frankly, I don't care."

"Neither do I," he said. "Fifty-five."

"Fine. We got that out of the way. I'm half your age," she teased.

"The hell you are. And if either one of us hears the body clock ticking, it's you."

"OK, OK, touché," she admitted. How did he know she had been feeling like time was getting away from her?

"Hey, we're not finished here," he added. "'Older man' is not how I would like to be described."

"Oo, you're touchy. You're about as bad as a black guy I once dated. I used the term descriptively, and he thought I was prejudiced."

"'Old' is not descriptive. Distinguished is descriptive."

"Ooh, so modest! Now I know what you think of yourself!" She twirled and wrapped herself in the phone cord.

"Well, I think I'm OK. It still amazes me when some woman – any woman, actually – seems to be admiring me. It doesn't happen very often."

"Probably a lot more often than you know." She took a breath and changed gears. "Can I speak frankly? I don't know if this – you and me talking and being … friends – is a very good idea. As a matter of fact, I'm pretty sure it's not a very good idea."

There was a pause, a long one. Had he been thinking about this, too? "Well, maybe not," he said, "but there are a lot of things I want to tell you, and you are going to listen, but not on the phone. So how about coffee this Saturday at two at …" and he named a favorite place in the Village.

Natalia tried briefly to resist, reluctantly said, "OK," and hung up, thrilled. She could hardly wait for Saturday to come, even though it was only two days away.

◆ ◆ ◆

The weekend seemed light years distant to Strong, so he tried to keep busy. Despite himself he thought of

Natalia constantly, to the point of distraction. His wife was going to Florida for a few days to visit her family, so he was free. He wasn't going to cheat on her, he never had and he wasn't going to start now. He was pleased when he took his wife to the airport that he stopped dreaming of the young woman he couldn't wait to see the next day. He was his usual, easy-going self with the woman beside him in the front seat of the car, the woman with whom he had, very happily, shared most of his life. As he drove, from the corner of his eye he saw she was looking at him occasionally, with a certain sardonic air. Could she possibly know? he wondered. Is there some secret, silent alarm for females that warns them when a mate is having wayward thoughts? It wouldn't surprise him. Women were different, that was for sure.

"Say 'hello' to your family for me."

"Right," she said, bundled up in a heavy coat and wool scarf against the rain and the cold.

"Wish I could go with you." He was trying.

"No, you don't. You don't like them. I don't blame you. They are a little weird, good ol' Mom and Dad." She turned the heat up one notch too many but he didn't say anything. "What are you going to do this weekend?" The windshield wipers went swish-swish, swish-swish.

He focused on the road ahead. "Nothing much, I guess." He wasn't sure if that was a lie or a prophecy.

"Stay out of trouble."

"What the hell is that supposed to mean?"

"Jeez. Touchy-touchy. It's not supposed to mean anything. Hey, have some fun."

"OK. Sorry."

They arrived at the terminal and Strong climbed out in the rain to help with her bag. She gave him a brief kiss. "Anyway, I love you," she said. She didn't wait for a response; she wasn't that kind of woman. He loved that about her.

"'Bye. Call me," he called after her as she disappeared through the sliding glass doors with a wave.

Strong took a breath, looking around. This is the real world, he reminded himself.

◆ ◆ ◆

Saturday came. Strong took the train in to New York, dressed in a jean shirt and slacks with a mid-length dark brown leather jacket. He had stood dressing in front of the full-length mirror in his bedroom far too long, considering what to wear. First he tried on a button-downed blue shirt that he usually reserved for important business meetings. It didn't look right. Too buttoned-down. Then he donned a mauve short-sleeved polo shirt with someone else's initials over the breast, and that didn't look right, either. He threw it on the bed with the button-down. He remembered doing the same thing in high school before his very first date, a sterile trip to the movies with a girl who made him feel so awkward he vowed he would never go out again.

Finally he said out loud to his image, "Oh, to hell with it," and wore what was comfortable. As luck would have it, he looked great. On the train, a girl at New Rochelle stopped in her tracks and started to sit next to him. His look scared her off. He was reserved.

Natalia was waiting for Strong at a table in the back of the café, her long legs crossed in fawn slacks. From a distance he could see she wore a brown suede jacket and caramel turtleneck. The colors were good on her. They matched the brown of her eyes and set off her dark coloring. Her eyes glistened, underscored by a slash of russet lipstick and a hint of makeup on a field of olive skin. Black hair tumbled down. Strong found it hard to believe he was meeting someone so striking.

The café was overheated, as if to compensate for the chill outside, where the leafless trees stood like black stakes jammed in the ground. As he made his way through the tables, he noted people reading, couples talking and stirring their tea. An elderly lady had a small fuzzy dog at her feet, its chin on its paws. It watched Strong and raised its head warily when he passed. When Strong stopped at Natalia's table he felt more awkward than the high school date. His hands were huge and hung lifeless. He didn't know what to do with them.

Natalia stood on tiptoe and gave him a kiss on the cheek. "Sit down. You look like you're about to croak," she said.

He laughed. "So much for pretenses," he said. "What would you like to do today? It's so beautiful out."

"Well, I would like to spend the whole day with you," she said with a very bright smile.

"You're on," he replied with a shiver. "Finish your coffee, and let's start with a walk."

◆ ◆ ◆

They ambled arm in arm, not speaking much. This was a strange, parallel universe apart from the rest of Strong's life. Natalia smelled of a hint of perfume. Her raven hair was caught by the wind. Every now and then she glanced at him, but most of the time she just walked along, taking in the street life around them, hanging lightly onto his arm.

"This is beautiful," he said after a bit, finally relaxing. He felt so alive. She held on and didn't say much. She watched as he looked in windows, pointed out things, smiled at people. They walked easily together, he noted.

This is so comfortable, he thought. She felt warm next to him. He tried to remain aloof and objective, without any success. She slowly edged closer. He talked less and less. Finally she leaned her head against his shoulder, and held his arm with both hands. He stopped talking altogether.

After another block of silence and she said, "Come with me."

◆ ◆ ◆

n her apartment she threw the key on the narrow side-board and turned to him with an open face. "Welcome to my world," she said, put her hands on his cheeks and pulled his face down. Her lips were deceptively soft and thick against his, and oddly cool. She pressed against him from tip to toe. He kept trying to breathe.

"Come here," she said, led him by the hand to the couch and drew him down. "I shouldn't be doing this, but you are so damned attractive. Make love to me. Please."

She filled his mouth. His heart was in his throat. He pulled away to take her all in, give her everything he had and more, if he could. He kissed her hair, her neck, grazed her face, kissed her lips, her eyes, felt her back, pressed her spine, raked her side with his fingers. That made her cry out. She had wrapped one leg around him and was hold-ing on for dear life. She was strong and lean and going out of her mind. Her passion built so quickly, he was sure she wouldn't know he was even there in a minute. He decided to forget everything and just do what he felt like. He reached down between her legs. She moaned and shiv-ered. The look in her eyes was glazed, dark, deep. He wasn't sure he could keep up.

When he pulled back, she came around and said, "Come here," again, got up from the couch and headed for the bedroom, pulling off her jacket and her turtleneck as she went. Her bare back was flawless. By the time he got his shirt off, she had stripped naked and was waiting for him to do likewise.

This time she controlled herself to let him catch up, which he did, before she took off again like a mare on a run in a field, taunting him to follow, which he did, and then turning and waiting for him to arrive, which he did, and then waiting for him to enter, which he did, and then not waiting for him at all any more, just bucking and kicking and coming and going and flying and crying and coming and coming and coming. Which he did, also.

At the end she fell asleep, exhausted. He couldn't close his eyes. He was so alive he vibrated. There was a sheen of sweat over her, which he gently blew away as he watched her doze fitfully. The lipstick and the makeup were gone. He had eaten them away. The black hair fell down the side of her face. Her eyelids fluttered in sleep. Her olive skin was soft and flawless. Her breasts were small and her belly flat. He wanted to devour her; to eat her; to possess her; to make her his; to take her inside him, where she already lived; tuck her into the rest of his heart, which she already occupied; put her there so she could never leave, so he could feel like this forever and ever and ever.

His journey down her body made it only halfway before she stirred and he buried his face deep against her. She pressed her hands against his head to hold him there and opened up completely. In a moment she was wild again. They went on for a very long while.

Finally, in the dark of the early evening, they lay back.

For her part, Natalia couldn't think at all, and rested her head on his chest. He smelled of sweat, which she liked. His skin was soft, and while his face was rough and angular, it was his hands that were so exceptional. They kneaded her and felt her and stroked her in a way she had never known, as if he saw with his fingers, and touched her deeply and forever. She felt as if he sculpted her with them, and that her body took a new shape because of his hands. He made her feel she was beautiful, which she had never believed. She had always felt awkward and unsure. Boys – and later, men – had sought her out because of raw passion, she was sure. They never looked at her the way Strong had, never touched her the way he did. She clung to him in appreciation, and carefully touched him. When he stood up like a trooper she burst out laughing. "Oh, my God!" she said, "Not again!" That made him laugh also.

He flipped her on her side, pushed her legs to her chest and slipped inside.

"Oh, oh, oh," was all she managed. This, this was going to be difficult. She didn't dare think the word "love" but the word "passion" was beating like a drum in her heart. She came again, and then again and again and said, "Will you stop this, please!" and laughed out loud.

If only I could, was all he could think.

◆ ◆ ◆

The next two days were a blur. They were not out of bed long. A man of caution, Strong threw it all to the wind and did anything that came to mind. When they went out for coffee he stood behind her, pressed against her as they waited to place their order at the deli counter. He put his hands in the rear pockets of her jeans and squeezed. She stopped midway through her order, but managed to finish, then turned around and pressed against him from chest to toe.

People stood back and watched, as if these two were about to explode. They were oblivious. At night when they made dinner in her tiny kitchen, he couldn't keep his hands to himself. They reached out on their own and touched her everywhere as she tried to cook. Natalia dropped a plate they didn't clean up until morning. She responded to every touch. She made him drunk like wine, and he kept drinking. He refused to think about tomorrow. She couldn't remember how to.

When they said good-bye, he felt like she had reached in between his ribs and ripped his heart right out of his chest. He went home to sleep it off, half hoping he could.

She ached for him before the door closed.

◆ ◆ ◆

When Strong's wife called from Florida to extend her trip, he was truly sorry.

"Dad's not feeling good — well, I guess I should say." She had learned to correct herself since he was such a stickler for grammar.

He had picked up the phone in the den, and looked out at the bleak winterscape through rain-streaked windows, mentally probing the edges of his heart while they talked. He had hoped her return would grab him mid-flight and pull him back to earth. Now she wasn't coming.

"Isn't there any way ..." he started to ask and then closed his mouth. They chatted on for a bit. Three times he started to press her to come home, but didn't. Finally there was nothing more to say and they hung up. He remained motionless for a long time, his hand on the phone.

His heart felt bruised, as if it had been manhandled over the last few days. A dull ache bubbled up each time he stumbled over Natalia in his mind. They had agreed not to talk for a week. Their affair was all wrong, for both of them. It wouldn't work; it shouldn't work. There was no future.

The trouble was, it was working all too well. Strong thought of every morsel of her, sorry that he had showered and could no longer catch her scent. His mind cruised her body like his hands, brushed against each part and watched it flinch and shiver. The thought of her made him ache. That night he had a solitary dinner in front of the TV. When someone mentioned Russia on the screen, his heart stopped cold.

Two days later Strong threw in the towel and called. It was 6:30 at night. He was in the city at his office. He never expected her to be home. She picked up on the first ring. "Are you OK?" he asked.

Natalia was so happy to hear from him she almost screamed. She put her fist in her mouth to hold it back, stomped once and then said, now under control, "Actually, not."

"Yeah, well if it's any comfort, me neither."

"God have I missed you!" she exploded.

"I can't even begin to tell you all the things I want to say," he said. "First, I want to thank you, and apologize for putting you in this situation, for making things difficult for you, for …"

"Oh, shut up!" she interrupted and stomped her foot again. She wanted to jump through the line and crawl into his mouth, wrap herself around his tongue, slip down his throat and squeeze his heart. Tears slid down her cheeks.

"You sound wonderful," he said with a great rush of relief. They were talking. She felt the same way he did. She wasn't toying with him. She meant it. He had been so worried.

"So do you." There was a pause. "Are you OK … at home?" she asked obliquely. She didn't want to say "wife," but she couldn't pretend she hadn't thought about it, either.

"My wife stayed in Florida with her family. Something about her dad being sick. So I'm home alone."

"Oh." He was home alone. It made her ache. If he were hers, he would never be alone. She didn't want to make love; she didn't want to do anything; she just wanted to be with him. I'm going nuts, she practically said out loud.

"Now it's my turn to thank you. I have never had such a … wonderful time in my life," she finished awkwardly, not knowing how to tell him he had set her hair on fire all over.

"I'll tell you what. Let's be sure it's not the only time," he said jocularly, without thinking. There was a silence and he realized that something was wrong. It was as if he had opened the wrong door.

She was confounded. How could it ever be the only time? How could it not be forever? How could he say that? What was he trying to say? Did he want out already?

He could feel her change without knowing exactly why. What was wrong?

"Right," she replied. The prick! He was just stringing her along – the bastard!

"Wait a minute," he said. "I think we got a little off-track there. I have been trying my best to put you out of my mind for the last two days – and failed miserably. Do you understand that?"

"I guess."

"You guess? What the hell are you talking about, 'you guess'?"

"I don't know. Listen, I have some work to do. I've got to catch up." She tapped her foot with a scowl on her face. How could she be so stupid? He was just using her. She was a convenient lay, a quick, hot roll in the hay. Fuck!

"Yeah, me too. That's why I called, to tell you I had a lotta work. Guess I'll just sit here, not answer the phones and work till I fall asleep at my desk. Gee, I'm so glad I called!"

"At your desk? You mean you're in the city?"

"Of course I'm in the city. Where did you think I was?"

"I thought you were home. Never mind! What are you doing at your office? Oh, forgive me; I can be so damn stupid! Why are you calling? Why aren't you here? How fast can you get here? I'll make dinner, I'll get wine, I'll, I'll, I'll …" He was here in the city! "Will you please get in a goddamn cab right now? Are you listening to me?"

He was.

When he walked in the door, she was short of breath. She looked at him a long minute, held off as long as she could and then flew at him, enfolded him like a sheet, tears wetting his shirt. God, why am I crying! she thought. She had him on the couch in a second. Her thought about not wanting to make love vanished instantly, replaced by raw passion. Sex left them both sweating and out of breath.

"I am so in love with you," he said evenly a little later as they lay entwined on the couch. She had her leg over his hip, and he could feel the dampness of her sweet spot.

He had never said that to anyone. Only rarely did he tell his wife he loved her, although he loved her a great deal. "I want to be sure you hear me when I say that. I don't say it lightly."

"I hear you just fine," she said with her head on his chest, looking south. She mulled over her feelings as she listened to this man who made her feel so whole, so alive, so vibrant, so poignant, so much a woman. But he was never going to be hers, to have in the morning and hold in the night, to cling to in the dark, to cry on and laugh with and live with for the rest of her life. She couldn't say she loved him back, although she ached to do so. Her heart felt crushed under the weight of her reluctance. It would have been such a relief to tell him, but that gift could only be given once, and now was not the time. How she wished it were.

"Can you stay the night?" That was the most she was willing to admit, that she wanted him to stay.

"Well, let's see," he said casually, faking it.

"You bastard!" she howled and pummeled his chest with her fists.

He held them tight until she stopped struggling and nestled into his chest. "Are you hungry? Dinner! You've never had a Russian dinner. I'm going to make you a real Russian dinner. Stay here. Don't move."

She leaped up, pulled a sweater over her sleek body, jumped into some jeans without any underwear and was gone, returning in twenty minutes with all sorts of things, not the least of which were vodka and caviar.

What was she doing? She never cooked for men. Sitting on the bed she poured the vodka and brought caviar with crackers and minced onion. Eventually they got to the table and dinner. The next day they both had a terrible headache. Neither regretted it in the least.

FIVE

Two Women

Strong hated duplicity, and he hated himself for it. How could he lead a double life? He had vowed never to conduct himself deceitfully, and now he was doing it full-tilt. It was as if he were two people, each going in their own, separate directions. Clearly it would tear him in half.

Natalia filled so much of him that every time they were apart he could feel her tug. His feelings for his wife were more subtle. They had spent so many years together, growing from lovers to friends who knew and understood each other completely; there was a force like gravity between them. They pulled together, shared everything, but passion had long since given way to habit and acceptance. What did he expect?

He knew men who thought this kind of contented relationship was a failure, men who left their wives for younger women as soon as they could afford it. He knew equally well that that was a terrible mistake. But now, sex was secondary to his wife. Sex didn't come naturally, of its own. She enjoyed it, but she never needed it. For her, its allure was fading. For him that light was still bright and burning. Now he saw both sides of the male-female-later-in-life equation, and he wasn't sure he could factor it all out. This was an unfamiliar formula. He wondered how it would tally.

On the surface, his new arrangement of awful duplicity seemed to be working. He cruised along, getting through the day with no problem and making it home through dinner in relative internal calm.

His wife was not oblivious, he was sure. He sensed she might have been thinking about their relationship for some time, but probably not with the urgency that gripped him. Surely she noticed something was different, perhaps lacking, but it wasn't critical, and he knew she didn't miss passion the way he did. She focused her attention on other things, instead. Friends were more important to her, and she had many. He had few. Business was fun, but not critical – she still sold a little real estate.

For him, business was damn near everything. His work was part of who he was, a large part, if truth be known. Advertising proscribed to a considerable degree the way he thought about himself and therefore the way he looked and the clothes he wore, the car he drove and even the place he called home.

Strong mulled these thoughts over at night with a glass of wine in his hand and a desire to pick up the phone in his heart. He and Natalia had agreed he wouldn't call from the country. There would be no furtive phone conversations from the den, no mixing of one life with the other, they decided. He had no idea where this ship was steaming, but he was unwilling, or unable, to disembark.

If nothing else, this affair had torn the face off Strong's complacency and made him take a hard, close look at who he was. He wasn't sure he liked what he saw. If he disappeared tomorrow, there would be damned few people who would remember him six months from now, save his wife and daughter. He wouldn't leave a big footprint in the sand.

What he kept stumbling over was the need for passion, for excitement. Natalia filled that niche to overflowing. She woke him up and heightened his senses till they tingled and his blood roared. He was wide awake now. When he was with her, when he thought about her, so many currents surged through him that he couldn't keep track of them all. He had always wanted to live life fully, and here, in this absurd duplicity with wife and lover, he was.

He was most concerned about feeling empty without Natalia, and showing it to his wife. At home he struggled to remember this was the life he had built for some twenty-plus years, and a damned good life it was. Few men still laughed heartily with their mates of such duration, but he did. Too many men seemed resigned to desiccated spouses who were bleached, thickened and sagging, with all the sex drained out of them. He suspected that some of these men were just marking time until they could afford a last hurrah.

Some women he knew were terrified their husbands would strike it rich and get the big promotion, afraid that with the job would come a new sports car, a girl half their age and a divorce, leaving them with the house, the mini-van and the kids. That scenario made them feel like concubines, whores to be discarded when they no longer performed or were needed.

Strong watched these women get hard around the edges. Their mouths turned down, despite the occasional face-lift. There was too much booze, but who could blame them for dulling the dread with something? Strong sympathized. What an awful prospect that your life could take a sharp turn so quickly, so completely, at the whim of someone else, that you could awaken one day and realize the partnership you had come to expect for eternity could be unilaterally canceled, an abandoned oar swinging listlessly in the oar lock and the boat going in circles as you rowed on alone. From that point it would be each man – and each woman – for himself. They had been partners, but now they would be foes. These women felt they had been cruelly cheated. More than one had told him so. Maybe they had been.

And they were all alone. There was no one to unload on – at least, they rarely did, as far as Strong could tell. He didn't blame them. To whom could they admit that once upon a time they actually believed that life was simple and straightforward, and that if they raised their kids right, kept the house neat, shaved their legs, were polite, sexy, observed the absurd dress rules at the club and had good friends – people with style and some values – that it would all work out fine, that they were safe? And then suddenly they discovered that they weren't safe at all. They would never tell anyone that. Shit! It meant the future could be literally anything. "Give me another drink."

Strong had thought a lot about this, and it made him feel bad. These women discovered that despite their best efforts, life happened around them, and they were god-damned stunned and powerless when the shit hit the fan. Following the rules was no guarantee, no guarantee at all. Was there really no home base, nothing solid and firm and unchanging, nothing you could always count on? Husband? Kids? Friends? No? Then, fuck it, why not have another drink? He didn't blame them one bit.

He wanted to tell these women that they had plenty of company, friends like him who would have understood completely, other women who harbored the identical feelings because they came out of the same Girls' School/College/Two-Years-In-New-York-And-Got-Married School Of Life. But he never did. It would have hit too close to home. They would have looked at him like he had just pawed through their underwear drawer. They avoided talking about the nastier realities of life, like the possibility of divorce. Divorce, and the resultant "diminished circumstances", brought social abandonment. It was a form of death, or so women thought. They would do almost anything to avoid it, just like prisoners on the way to the gallows. They would scream, cry, cheat, beg, lie, steal – anything.

He had seen women get frantic when the big job came down the pike and put their husband in the Big Leagues. They could tell because he suddenly started acting differently, with a new absurd swagger, and maybe even an ascot at the club. They bought the new house or vacation hideaway or something to recharge themselves and involve their mates, anything to keep their men interested and their marriage together. The smart ones realized if a patched-together life was so easily endangered, maybe it wasn't worth keeping in the first place. Some of them, the bolder ones, shocked their men, sitting down at breakfast on a weekend morn saying, "You know, this isn't working. It hasn't worked for quite a while. Let's stop kidding ourselves and get a divorce. I don't even know you any more. And you have no idea who I am. More coffee?"

Then they moved out and sold real estate or got remarried in California or South Carolina or Florida, leaving their men astounded and alone, wondering what the hell they had done, what had gone wrong. Sweet Jesus, they were just trying to keep up with everything themselves, keep ahead of the other wolves at the office, and stay in front of the pack so they didn't get eaten. What had they done wrong? What was with these women? What did they really want? Shit!

That was the point. No one had done anything particularly wrong. There was just an accumulation of things they hadn't done right. Sometimes the abandoned husbands tried to patch it up, go back and repair the past, but usually when things had gotten this far the marriage was a goner, and both parties discovered that the person who for so long had been so close was now a stranger, or worse. On the phone with each other they felt they were talking through a thick slab of glass. After a while they didn't return each other's calls. That life was dead.

Strong hated the whole syndrome, most of all when he saw beautiful young women whom he found attractive, despite himself. To throw away so many private, intimate moments because his wife simply followed the rules of nature and grew older, seemed cruel and heartless in the extreme. Age was something he had to accept, to live with, he told himself.

He envisioned, briefly, a new life without her. He couldn't bear to imagine the details of telling his wife he would leave or what it would do to Shelley, so he skipped that part. A romantic, he projected the future. He would move to the city, they would get a loft in the Village or SoHo, someplace radically different, a completely new start. He would be a new man, feel ten years younger, wear jeans, and walk with a spring in his step. Each night they would go out to some corner bistro or Italian family restaurant, where everyone would see they were in love and treat them with deference. He would reach across the red-checked tablecloth and caress her face. She would look steadily at him, and when they went home, she would undress and not hang up her clothes and lie back on the bed, inviting him to do again what they had done so well so many times before.

He wasn't stupid. He knew that wouldn't last, that sooner or later the veneer would wear thin and they would live an ordinary, everyday life, but he didn't really believe it. No, they would go on being happy forever until one day on the street, on a plane or at a party, over the canapés and the cocktails, he would hear, "Hello, Ben," and he would turn around and it would be his wife with another man. He'd say, "Hi," as if it were a pleasant surprise, but it wouldn't be. There would be cursory introductions, she might even say, "I would like you to meet my husband," and he would feel like he was in another world that looked the same but wasn't, a world in which he should have a place but didn't, with a woman who knew everything he thought, everything he felt, understood him to the core, and if not, understood him damn well, a woman who had spent much of her life looking through his eyes, and he through hers, and now they were separate, apart, severed completely like Siamese twins sliced apart, and instead of seeing as one they were two, no matter how he might wish it wasn't, and after a few more inconsequential remarks and pleasantries from her, with awkward silence from her new man, she would be off and he would be left standing there knowing, without the slightest doubt in the world, that when he had walked away he had made a wrong turn, gone the wrong way, left her and a good part of himself behind when he never should have, and that there was no going back. There were few times in life when you knew without doubt you had gone wrong, and this would have been one of them. He had ruined a large portion of his life, maybe all of it, and if he wanted to know the reason, he had only to look in the mirror.

And yet here he was, dreaming of a woman much younger, more passionate, and so beautiful. And he had thought he was smart. What a fool!

The next time they met in the city, Natalia was bright and cheery and a little distant. Strong was unsure where the relationship would go next.

They had lunch with wine at a dark, Westside basement restaurant replete with red banquettes and haughty waiters. Strong's desire surfaced halfway through his first glass. She never wore a bra, and he wanted to reach across the table and touch her nipple. He didn't honestly care who saw, which was crazy. He had acquaintances all over the city. Eventually someone was going to see them together.

For her part, she enjoyed his discomfort. She could tell she was working on him, and she liked it. She kept her legs tightly crossed and calculated how long it would take to get to her apartment by cab. When she got up to go to the ladies' room, she brushed against him as she passed. When she came out, he was waiting at the cabstand. They made it to her place in ten minutes flat.

◆ ◆ ◆

At home one evening, his wife stumbled as she walked into the kitchen and almost dropped the plates. He didn't think much of it, and neither did she. A week later, she got out of bed and fell flat on her face.

"Jesus, honey, are you OK?" Strong asked, sitting up in bed, wide-awake. She must have tripped.

"Fine, fine," she said, recovering. She disappeared into the bathroom. He wondered.

Three days later, he got a call midday at the office. "You better come home. Something is wrong." He dropped the phone, told his secretary to cover for him and headed straight for the train.

When he got to the doctor's office, she was sitting in the waiting room. She was a strong, handsome, compassionate woman, but she looked small and frightened and frail. He put his arms around her and held her close. She looked up at him and tried to keep a bright face, but there were tears running down her cheeks.

After the doctor spoke with him, Strong understood why. "Come on, let's get out of here," he said to her, and they left.

Not a lot of time – that was the long and the short of it. Cancer could be like that. He felt his whole world swing on a hinge. Natalia in the city suddenly shrank, as if she had been shoved to the distant horizon. He never called her.

◆ ◆ ◆

When Strong and his wife had first met – he was a budding journalist – he had thought she was tight-lipped, remote and passionless like other American women he had known. Enjoyment didn't seem to be a part of their make-up. Physically, she was blessed with strong legs, a full chest and a handsome face, but she had been reserved, cautious. He could never imagine her liking sex, just letting fly, enjoying it as much or more than he did.

But then one day they had begun talking about this and that, and to his surprise she was quite different. She listened and told him honestly what she thought; not what he wanted to hear, but what she thought. He liked that. It pushed him back, stood him up and made him take another look.

She was not from the East. She was from out West where there were fewer restrictions, fewer social dos and don'ts. Westerners hadn't had time to form all the rules and regulations. They were too busy simply surviving. They said what they thought.

She told him she would like to go skiing with him, and she made no qualifications, like "with friends" or "for the day". He realized she meant there would be a lot more to the outing than skiing. He liked that.

One evening as they were having dinner at a place he couldn't afford she said, "You're a strange man." There was linen on the table. He hadn't eaten off a tablecloth in some time. Young journalists were cheap, in line with their pay, but she warranted linen and good wine.

"How do you mean?" The comment didn't offend him. He rather liked her guts to make it.

"You're blunt, but you are also quite sensitive."

"A brute who likes art." They had actually talked about Impressionism on the second coffee date.

"Exactly. First non-gay guy I've known who loves art."

"How do you know ..." he teased, "... for sure?" He was referring to the gay part of her comment. So far it had been a chaste relationship. Strong had decided he was going to keep his hands in his pockets as long as he could. He wanted to see what she would do.

"I know," she said. "Oh, I know."

Later that night, with her leading the way and conducting very nicely, they made love the first time and it had been very good, really smooth and natural, and she had fallen asleep first. He had to laugh. This woman was going to be different.

Two months later he proposed. It wasn't as awkward as he thought it would be, no down-on-his-knee, will-you-be-mine-forever silliness, a memory that would have forever appalled him. They were cooking veal for dinner in the kitchen of his stubby studio flat in Albany, where he had the newspaper job. Each had a glass of jug white wine. He was at the stove, sautéing.

"So, I've been thinking ... " he had started, stirring.

"That's OK," she said, sitting legs crossed in snug jeans at his chrome and Formica kitchen table. Her dark brown hair was gathered back with a yellow ribbon that matched the tabletop. Her lipstick was bright and perfect. She had a way of doing it all right without making a big deal of it. One leg was bouncing.

"OK, no fooling now. I have been thinking about you and me."

"Oh ..."

"I want to know what you think, but I've been thinking that we just seem to be getting closer and closer, we talk better and better, and the natural outcome of that is to ... is to ... " He turned around to look at her. She waited patiently for the shoe to drop. "... get married."There, he had said it. It didn't sound too foreign.

"I agree," she said immediately.

"You do?"

"Yes."

"Boy, that was fast."

She laughed. "Somehow I thought you might ask me this weekend."

"You did? How would you know that?"

"I haven't the slightest idea, but I did. It just came out of nowhere."

"God, that's scary."

"Don't worry. Are the mushrooms all right?"

Another two months and they were married. It had always seemed absolutely right except for one moment on their honeymoon when he had looked across the dinner table and thought, for just a second, What in hell am I doing here?

She had spotted it immediately. "Are you all right?"

He pulled out of it. "Yeah, fine." Later she confessed to him that three days earlier she actually started packing a bag to flee the country, then took a deep breath and settled down. That made him feel a whole lot better.

◆ ◆ ◆

Their first serious test came a year after they were married. Shelley hadn't arrived, in fact was seven months away. His wife had just started to show. The apartment had been too small so they rented a tiny house down by the tracks above the gray-running river. It was all they could afford. The one saving grace was the Hudson through the thick maple trees in the backyard of the white saltbox house. Otherwise it was a neighborhood of broken cars, abandoned tricycles, and Saturday night fights. Neither of them imagined that they would be there for long. Older couples lived on either side, nice people who smoked and idled the days away in bored retirement.

Strong was the police reporter who also covered City Hall. He got an occasional shot at a statewide story from the capital when someone went on vacation and his editors asked him to fill in. It was heady stuff, talking to the big politicians – powerful, confident men and the occasional woman whose names were known in every household throughout the state. He was excited when they stopped mid-stride in the marble hallways and took his questions. He felt important.

But most of the time it was up a 4 AM, dawn still two hours distant, driving to police stations in the cold or the rain – sometimes snow – to sort through reports from the night before for a tasty tidbit of murder, mayhem or malfeasance. These he would call in to the newsroom, then drive to the paper to flesh them out on a typewriter. By noon his head was usually drooping over his desk. Most of the other reporters had yet to come in, particularly those on political beats. At 1 they let him go home.

So it was with some anticipation that he took on a temporary assignment to cover the upcoming mayoral election. He had no idea this was a journalistic mine field.

The race hinged on a typical upstate New York boondoggle – construction contracts. Highways were big moneymakers, and who won the contracts was always suspect.

He quickly learned you weren't supposed to ask too many questions about these things.

The mayor, a hefty Italian woman with a mustache, took him into her confidence.

"You're new here, right, Strong? It is Strong, isn't it?"

"Yes, Madame Mayor."

"You certainly didn't hear it from me, but I wouldn't get too curious about highways, if you know what I mean. It won't be good for anybody."

"I don't know what you mean," he had replied dead-pan. He really didn't.

"Well, you'll find out." That sank the hook in.

That night at home he could hardly sit still at the dinner table. His wife listened but didn't say much. "Better talk to someone at the paper about this," she finally advised. "I think I'll get a job."

"Oh, come on," he said. "What are you saying?"

"Nothing, really. I'm getting bored. I need to work." She took a position as office assistant for a local real estate company within the week.

Strong started digging. Damned if he was going to be told what to do by some small time politician. He was going to find out what was what. He was going to do a hell of a job as an investigative reporter, he was going to expose something big and maybe even get a Pulitzer. *The New York Times* would beg him to join their staff.

Of course, what he found out was that the mayor's only major opponent had all sorts of shady connections to state highway contracts, and the mayor was squeaky clean. He duly reported what he discovered. No one cared. The mayor won the election. She stopped him in the City Hall basement two weeks later.

"Hey, Strong. Thanks for the lift. You should have looked into the new airport." Then she guffawed. It turned out her finger prints were all over the half billion-dollar project that the City Council had approved. All her cronies benefited. Strong was devastated. He had been blindsided. He felt completely stupid. One day he came home before noon.

"Aren't you home early?"

"I quit," he said and slammed the bedroom door. His downward spiral lasted a year. His wife kept quiet as long as long as she could. Then one afternoon, home exhausted from work, she exploded.

"Get your goddamned ass in gear," she hollered. They moved to the city, she took a job in Soho real estate for which she had a considerable flare, and kept them afloat for another year while he staggered and flailed, trying to find a niche. Advertising was a complete fluke. Drinking at a bar one Thursday afternoon, his inebriated stool mate said he should get into it.

"Oh yeah, why?" Strong asked.

"I dunno. You were a newspaperman, you can write, you're cute and what can you lose? We got an opening at our agency." He put his arm around Strong's shoulder in a way that made Strong feel uncomfortable. The next day, Strong got the job copywriting. Three years later he got fired for telling the boss, a real jerk who had the answer to everything, to go fuck himself. Strong started his own agency, consisting of himself and a phone in a closet of their flat. He would take Shelley to nursery school in the morning, then plead for a chance to pitch an idea to companies he cold-called all day until he picked her up in the afternoon. Once again his wife stood by him as he struggled for what seemed like forever. Finally he got someone to listen. They were his first clients – a parking management company – and in time he could afford an office, then an assistant, then an "art department" of one, until in twenty years he actually had a name that was recognized on Madison Avenue. Whenever he thought about it, he was a little amazed that it had happened at all. He would occasionally burst out laughing at his good fortune over a drink on the train out to the country.

Strong and his wife were happy for quite a long time, did all the good things and enjoyed each other thoroughly. From lovers they grew to become friends, best friends, the kind that could listen and then finish each other's sentences. The kind that could yell at each other and bruise the parts without damaging the whole, although sometimes they came damned close. They thought on the same wavelength. If she liked something, she asked him what he thought, not for his approval but for his opinion, which she respected. She might agree or not.

Passion cooled as it always does, but the friendship got better. Sex was pretty easy, fairly often and very good. He was periodically surprised by her frankness. "I didn't like that much," she said over the stove after he once had tried something new in bed, and then she went on cooking. He suspected it was an exceptional marriage. How could he truly know? And now she was going.

SIX

PRECIOUS TIME

Strong worked half days. He and his wife were going to make the most of the time remaining. She faced her own devils quietly and with increasing determination. As for him, he felt like his face was pushed up against the window of reality, so that he would be sure to take a very good look.

It happened fast. In a few weeks, she was noticeably thinner. When friends came by, they tried not to appear shocked, but they were. Before long they didn't come by at all. His wife seemed to understand quite well, and took it with a grain of salt.

"It scares them," she informed him. "They didn't think they were mortal. I didn't think I was either, for that matter. Now they realize they are. Some of them may even get angry, and they won't know why." Strong had noticed one or two harsh looks from acquaintances in the village, and now he understood. He admired her perception.

To his surprise, she never got angry herself, as all the experts said she should – angry at the abrupt pivot in the course of her life; angry that she wouldn't see grandchildren, ever; angry that they wouldn't hike in Switzerland together as they had promised; angry they wouldn't sell this house and get another to decorate the way they always wanted; angry that they wouldn't ride horses in the rain; angry that the train would be pulling out of the station and he would be on it, and she would not, angry that she would be left standing alone on the empty concrete platform, watching the last light of the last car disappear from view. Life would go on. She wouldn't be there to enjoy it.

She might not have been angry, but he sure as hell was. Where was the justice in all this? What the hell had she done except live as well as she could, which was damned well in his estimation, and had been kind and nice and pretty funny and damned bright? When he pondered a world without her, a great lump grew in his throat and an awful pressure ballooned in his chest. He began to see clearly that there were many things he had taken for granted, and that these things were often the most important of all, starting with life itself. He didn't know anyone who was thankful for each breath they took, each day they awoke anew. Ironically, she now was. When he told her this, she laughed and said, "What did you expect?"

They took their evening meals together, she with her soup and he with the latest from the frozen dinner department. It tasted fine to him. A glass of wine made it even better. She had a glass, too, despite doctor's orders.

"Doctors forbid everything that's a pleasure in life, if they think you're really sick," she said with a laugh. "May I have another glass of wine, please?"

She read much of the day, propped up in bed in a quilted house jacket, occasionally looking out the window at the woods beyond the back lawn. She had always loved the woods, even when they were stark and cold as they now were in their "winter dress", as she called it. He had always seen death in the bare limbs, and she had always seen life in the knowledge of the coming spring with new leaves and shoots. She seemed to, still. For him that was impossible. There wasn't going to be any spring. Soon there would be no tomorrow, much less spring. He felt the knife of disappointment, bitterness, and sorrow twist deep inside. He was ashamed when it cut hard in him and tears welled up in his eyes. He would excuse himself and leave the room.

She knew perfectly well what he was doing, and that it was a battle he had to win by himself. She said, just once, "It's not so bad."

"Speak for yourself," he shot back, regretting it the moment it was out of his mouth.

When Shelley came home, it was almost more than he could bear. She tried to maintain a happy face, but when she saw her mother, her skin gray, her eyes sunken, she collapsed like a stack of poker chips on a table. Shelley buried her head in the covers while her mother stroked her hair.

That night, Shelley left. Before going, she said, "Mom, I want to remember you the way you have always been to me – young, happy, vibrant, strong and <u>mine</u>. And I know that soon you are not going to be any of these things, and I can't bear it. I have to go. I love you with every bit of my heart and a great deal more. Oh shit!" She stomped her foot. "Life is never going to be the same for me again."

Tears streamed down her cheeks. She kissed her mother, hugged her again, gave her father a kiss and a hug, and left. It was the only time he saw his wife close to tears in those last days.

Later, as he stood in their bedroom door, she asked, "What is it about two people that makes them close?" after their daughter had left.

"You mean, like you and Shelley?" he asked. He was headed for the kitchen with a tray of dirty dishes. She had barely touched her soup.

"Yes, and like you and me," she replied.

"Oh," he said. This was going to take some thought. He put the tray down beside him as he settled to the floor with his back against the door. "Well, about you and Shelley, I think it's something natural. She was a part of you, and then she popped into this world but she never stop being a part of you."

For an instant he remembered how exhausted she had looked in the hospital bed after twelve hours of labor. Drawn though she had been, her eyes glowed. He smiled. "At least, that's the way I feel about her," he said, returning to the present. "She is probably the only person I would die for without thinking about it. I had no idea I would ever feel that way about someone. It came as quite a surprise," he said.

His wife looked at him with a smile at the corners of her mouth. "I think you're right. How else could we have put up with some of the crap she gave us?" she asked.

He had to laugh at that one, then pulled at his jaw. "Now, about you and me. Let me see … " He leaned back, looking down, thinking.

"Well, OK, here is what I think," he said finally, playing with a spoon from the tray. "Nothing written in concrete here, but …you were the first woman I felt I could say absolutely anything I had on my mind to, and not be worried about the consequences. That really struck me. I remember going out with lots of girls …"

"I bet you do," she interjected.

"Now don't give me a ration of shit here, I'm trying to be sincere."

"Sorry." She plucked at the covers.

"OK. As I was saying before I was rudely interrupted, you were unique because I wasn't worried about the consequences of being myself. I wasn't thinking, 'Will she be offended? Will she be hurt?' I knew I could just say it."

That had been quite a revelation to him, he remembered. He had hated having to hold back, not be himself, unable to relax and enjoy the moment. Before her, it seemed women damned easily took offense at things he said or did, particularly when they were crazy about him and he wasn't nuts about them. They peered at him as if they were trying to see inside, as if what was on the surface wasn't the real him. He wasn't a subtle man. They made it so complicated. What they saw was what they got, like it or not. Then they would act hurt unless he changed, said he loved them, or pretended. He was not going to do that, and he never did. Most of his relationships had been brief.

"Was that good, just being able to be yourself? Is there a compliment hidden in there somewhere?"

"As a matter of fact, there is. It means that you were strong enough to take any of the crap I might put out, intended or not. And I can apparently put out a whole lot of crap."

"This is a very revealing conversation."

"Hah-hah. You asked a question, I'm giving you the answer. Do you want to hear it or not?" He was trying to sound gruff, but he was starting to crumble inside. So many of the things he had successfully bottled up were now bubbling to the surface. And he had thought he had it all under control. What a joke!

"Sorry again." She looked at him. "Are you OK?"

He ignored the question. "OK, so that's the first thing — someone who allows you to be yourself," he said and cleared his throat to get back on top.

"That's good. I like that. I agree."

How can she be so bright, so clear, so sharp? he wondered. "Good. Well, I've reached first base, but where do I go now? You know, you can jump in here anytime you want. This doesn't have to be a monologue."

"We'll see. You're doing pretty well on your own." She fiddled with the covers again.

"Thank you. Second thing is – what the hell is the second thing?"

She smiled. "Someone you like? I mean, really like? Even admire?"

"Yes, yes – absolutely. Someone you like as a friend, and admire as a person. I admired you for your individuality. You could be a Democrat, but vote against welfare – I dunno, something like that. You were always your own person."

"I'm not sure I like the verb tense you're using here."

"Oh come on, lighten up. That's the way you would say it no matter ..."

"Forget it. Bad job. Glimmer of self-pity there," she said, and looked down.

"Goddamn well due some," he said, and came off the floor. "This is so damn unfair." He put his arms around her and held her carefully. She was so frail. She felt brittle. Through the bay window next to her bed he could see the rain pouring down. The bare trees glistened in the light from the house.

She pushed him off. "Back to our talk. We were getting somewhere."

Strong sat on the bed and tried to be unemotional. "What else makes people close?" he asked rhetorically. "Well, I can't think of anyone I trust the way I trust you. I don't always agree with you ..."

"Tell me about it!" She clapped her hands. They made a soft sound, as if she wore mittens.

"But, goddamnit, I trust you are always honest with me, telling me what you think, without any so-called agenda. I'm right there, aren't I?"

"Oh, I don't know. Sometimes we women have an agenda, without which you men would never get where you want to go."

"What the hell is that supposed to mean?"

"It means sometimes if you aren't led by the nose, you will never get where you want to go in the first place."

"Oh, yeah? Like where? " He thought maybe he should be angry.

"I don't know. Foreign films, for Pete's sake. You always want to go to some idiot action movie and I have to finagle you into going to a foreign film you end up loving. Every time."

"Well ..." he said. "I don't disagree. OK. Let's wrap this up. One more thing. It's getting late ... "

"One more thing that makes you really close to someone ..." she mused out loud. "Physical attraction?"

"That's an interesting point. I don't think so." He was shocked at his own answer, but it was true. "I mean, sure, physical attraction counts for something at the beginning.

At least it's important not to be physically repulsed by someone. But the physical thing gets old after awhile, doesn't it? I mean, sex is never going to be as breathtaking as the first few times around. It's important that it's enjoyable and all, but I don't think it's going to move the earth every time. It would be a mistake to expect that, clearly. Hemingway set a great goal, but it's not one you're going to achieve too many times in life."

"We got there once or twice."

"You know, I knew something was special the first time we made love. No one – I mean no one – had ever fallen asleep before me afterwards. That was a surprise."

"I did?"

"Yep. Went to sleep like a baby."

"I don't remember."

"Of course not – you were asleep. It made me laugh." Was she blushing?

"Well, whatever it is that makes people close, I can't think of how we could have been closer and still been on Earth. I pretty much know you inside and out, good and bad."

"Bad? What are you talking about?" he said in mock indignation.

"Hey, if there weren't any bad, the good would be pointless." She fluffed her pillow and continued, "That's all I'm going to say right now. I'm tired. Get out of here. I love you."

"Me, too. Good night."

"Good night, life partner," she said, rolling over and fluffing her pillow once more.

"Life partner? Where the hell did that come from? You make me feel like a swan. They mate for life. We men are rogues, you know."

"Stuff it. You're not so bad. You are my life partner, and you damn well know it." She was settling into sleep with her back to him.

"Yes. Yes, I do. Thank you. Sleep tight. And by the way, I love you, too."

"I know that."

That was another thing that made people close, he thought as he closed the door quietly. They knew the other loved them.

He didn't go into work the next day. He sat with her and didn't say much. He was beginning to realize just how much they had together, and how valuable it was. It was wonderful. It was paradise. Suddenly the shortening time didn't make much difference. He kept smiling at her.

She looked at him quizzically, but didn't ask.

A cloud had lifted. There was only now, today, this evening, and this night. Tomorrow would take care of itself. He was so grateful.

That night when he brought the soup, she was turned to the window, which was streaked with rain again. Outside, the trees glistened in the cold. There was going to be a freeze.

He felt the chill through the windowpanes. He started to say something, but stopped and looked at her. The woods must have been the last thing she saw, he realized. A small smile lit her face. A book lay open on her lap, as if she had put it down to take a nap.

"Goddamnit. Goddamnit! We aren't finished talking!" he shouted, and hurled the tray against the wall. She hadn't even called him to say good-bye.

He sat on the bed, pressed her palm to his lips and broke down completely. Tears sprang from his eyes and poured down his cheeks. How could he have ever thought of someone else, let alone been obsessed? He couldn't even remember what Natalia looked like. Were all men so foolish? Already he missed his wife more than he ever thought possible. He felt as if the floor had opened up beneath him and he had fallen through, headlong. How could this be the same room, the same house? Half of him was gone.

Strong looked into her face, hoping she would suddenly awake, make a face and force him to laugh at his own foolishness, as she had done so many times before. But she ignored him, lying placid and immobile. For the first time, she was out of reach.

He felt her hand cool as he held it, wet with tears. He had always seen life as opening up before him, each day new and different. He would get up, go out, and meet it. She was always behind him. They were so close; he took for granted she would be there when he turned around. How stupid! Now it was ending. She was dropping away like a parachutist spread-eagled and fading far below, while he flew helplessly on, watching her disappear in the mist. He wanted to jump.

Well, buster, I guess it's time for you to learn: Sentences don't run on forever. There is always a period at the end. His body curled in anguish.

◆ ◆ ◆

The next days were a blur. How he got through them he never knew. Shelley came home and did everything, so he wouldn't have to think. He was thankful for that.

Strong couldn't get drunk, despite some serious efforts. He kept seeing his wife everywhere, expecting her to breeze in from the kitchen when he walked in the door, to roll over and touch him softly in the night, to be there when he mixed a drink, to close the door in his face when he tried to talk to her in the bathroom. She never was. Little sounds, once a smell in the kitchen, a song – he had even shouted sitting on the toilet for her to get the phone when it rang and then laughed at himself, just before he cried. God, was life nothing but a country and western song?

Friends came and went, meaning well. There was a service and a reception. When he came home and the front door slammed, it sounded like eternity closing behind him. For so many years he had forgotten how lonely he could feel, thanks to her. Now he remembered.

His office manager told Strong not to come to work, which was fine with him. He stayed away a month. They called him on important things, faxed him, sent him e-mail. He said 'yes' to everything. The house quickly lost a woman's touch – cut flowers, fresh fruit, watered plants, fluffed pillows arranged just so. He had taken it all for granted. Now he missed every one. Why didn't I see all this before, he asked himself. Unable to do such things properly, he didn't try. The house became cold, hollow, unlived-in. He threw out all the flowers. The warmth was gone. How true, he thought.

Strong looked in the mirror, and saw how much he had changed. His salt-and-pepper hair was mostly salt. There was a resignation around the eyes. Age spots bloomed overnight on the backs of his hands. He kept up his jogging routine desultorily, but at night he had an extra drink and often went to bed buzzing. The mornings were awful. Some days he didn't make it out of bed until noon.

Finally Shelley called and gave him a kick in the butt. "OK, she's dead. We both know that. Are you?" she demanded to know.

This from the daughter who had nearly exploded in grief at the funeral. Boy, they sure have comeback potential, these women, he thought.

"I resent that," he said defensively.

"Oh, give me a break," she shot back. "You need to get back in the game."

"Who the hell is this? You sound like my high school coach." he said. There was something familiar about all this.

"Damned straight. Go to work tomorrow."

"Oh, shit, all right. Don't call me."

"We'll see," was her parting threat.

SEVEN

BACK IN THE GAME

His first day back in the office, everyone was polite. Strong felt stiff, out of place, as if he were wearing a suit and tie for the first time. Worse, he felt old. He hid in his office most of the day. There were no calls. Not one.

The second day was better. He emerged from his office twice and spoke to someone. He had one call from a salesman asking him to switch the agency's long distance service. He stared at the phone until he realized his secretary had put it through to wake him up, give him something to do.

After a couple of weeks, Strong was as tired of his morose mood as the employees. By the end of the month, he almost wanted to get back in the swing of things. He was bored eating hot dogs for lunch from the sidewalk vendor all by himself. He could only handle so much mustard, onions, kosher beef and self-pity. All of them had their limitations.

At a staff meeting two weeks into the second month, Strong tentatively offered to make a pitch the following Tuesday. Who was going to refuse him? He was the boss.

They all cheered. His office manager did a little dance. Everyone was glad he was back. So, come to think of it, was he.

Pretty soon, work started to feel good again. He walked down the hall and popped into people's offices just to chat, which was unlike him. He was surprised he felt so open. At first the office veterans were wary, but that quickly wore off.

He was also surprised he had absolutely no desire to call Natalia. Quite the opposite: The idea repulsed him. His life had been ripped in half, and it was too painful to think about the half he had lost. She was part of it, and it was over, done and gone.

◆ ◆ ◆

As he rode home on the train at night, somewhere around Greenwich he would remember that he would eat dinner alone again tonight, and he had to look out the window so people couldn't see his face. The clink of solo silverware and no one to talk to was much more than he could bear. Once he had even taken down two plates as he prepared to serve, then stared at them until the food was cold. He threw it out and went up to bed.

He started going out. Anything to get away from that empty dining table. Local restaurants made their money from strong drinks, not good food. He did his best to appreciate the fare of breaded stuff with French names served by a hopeful waitress. He took a paperback to read during his meals. He hated the drive home afterwards, remembering things, silly things like fights they had had coming down the driveway, fights about nothing, mulish-ness on his part and truculence on hers, both lubricated by wine, or the time they stopped to watch raccoons dig up the garden and didn't do anything to frighten them, despite the havoc the little beasts were causing. Maybe he should sell the house. There was just too much of them together there.

Word quickly got around that Strong was eating out, and the invitations started, first a trickle and then a flood. At first, he was surprised and appreciative. He never had been close to any of these hostesses or their husbands, and now they were going out of their way to welcome him to dinner. They felt sorry for him. He didn't mind. He was grateful. They were being nice. There was not a lot of nice in the world, and he welcomed it when he found it. His appreciation gave him pause. Maybe he was changed by his experience.

He brought wine to these affairs, feeling awkward standing alone at the door with the bottle in one hand, ringing the bell and waiting for the door to open. His hosts all greeted him effusively and never mentioned his wife. Most were couples that seemed to do everything in pairs, like wearing shirts and playing golf or tennis. Strong and his wife had always done things separately. He jogged; she rode. He surfed; she sailed. So it had been, and they both liked it that way.

There was usually an extra woman at these dinners, and after a drink or two, she looked at him like he was dessert. It wouldn't have been so bad if they had been attractive to him, but they weren't, although they had tasteful dresses and jewels, with nothing ostentatious, no slit dresses or deep cleavage. He just wasn't in the game. He had lost his appetite. He felt sorry for them. They must be desperate and lonely, he thought.

When they saw he pitied them, they became furious. Several turned on him in the foyer as they left when the evening was over and, speaking carefully so as not slur their words, let him know they thought he was a prick. They didn't like being pitied. He didn't mean to offend, but there it was.

Once someone's daughter, about 26, spent a good part of the evening talking to him. She wore a short black dress and tall heels with bare legs, even in winter, but Strong quickly put her out of his mind. He could hear the whispers if he acted on that impulse – shock and disgust all around. People would have clucked approval if she had been one of the proffered dinner dishes, but here he would have been reaching for forbidden fruit. Recovery in sub-urbia didn't work that way. He couldn't have a great mar-riage, lose his wife and then reinvent himself with a girl half his age. "It wasn't done," is how the social arbiters at the club would have put it, which of course meant that all the men secretly wanted to do it and all the women were scared shitless they might.

This young girl looked good to him, but he could see she wasn't worth the price. He wasn't serious anyway. What was he thinking? His wife had been gone just a few months. How he missed her! There was hole in his heart through which the emotions drained out and he could feel nothing. She probably would have agreed that this young girl was the first woman worth looking at twice. His wife always had a knack of making a judgment without taking it personally. For the first time, Strong laughed out loud on the way home. God, he missed her, her unfailing friend-ship, her honesty, her humor. He ached.

◆ ◆ ◆

Out of the blue one evening, Strong got a call from Shelley. "Dad, I'm getting married!"

He was delighted for her. Her longtime boy friend was a nice kid who worked hard at his job, although Strong never quite understood what it was — something about computer languages. Strong wasn't clear what those were.

He took a sip of his drink. "Now wait just a goddamn minute," he said in mock gruffness. "No gal o' mine" – he was into his second martini – "is taking up with a young computer nerd."

"Dad, stuff it. You've been drinking."

"Yeah, so what?" He was in the living room, walking around in front of the empty fireplace and talking on the cordless. "Anyway, congratulations. I want to buy you the dress. Your mother would have insisted." He took another sip. He suspected he might have said "congrachelations", but he didn't care. He was proud of his daughter.

"Hey, you're going to buy me a whole hell of a lot more than the dress! Mom would have demanded!"

"I can see you have a new arrow in your quiver. Whenever there is a financial question, I am going to be shot through with something about your mother. I must plot an appropriate defense," he said grandly, slurring his words slightly and walking around the living room spilling his drink. This was fun. He might even take up smoking again.

She told him the details, explained his part and hung up. He was pleased she had become such a good coach and captain.

In truth, Strong was excited and sad at the same time. He was excited because Shelley's upcoming marriage was something new. It felt like new life, and he needed that. There had been too much death around him – his wife, of course, but the barren winter trees, the hapless dinners out, the sad mis-matches at every dinner party, the Russian girl who had once sent him through the roof, all losses.

But he was happy for Shelley, for although he didn't understand her fiancé, he suspected the fellow was all right, and clearly they were very comfortable with each other.

To hell with passion, Strong thought to himself, freshening his martini. If you're not comfortable with someone, life's exhausting. For the first time in a very long while, he saw Natalia's face in his memory. For so long, she had been faceless, nearly nameless. Their affair was a remote memory. He realized that to cook on all four burners, to be fully aflame, to be on fire as she made him, was exciting but exhausting as well. There was no time to take a breath. He would get worn down having to be constantly on his guard, playing a game, trying to stay ahead, thrusting and parrying and working it all to the hilt. It looked good in the movies for Cary Grant, but damned if it worked for him.

At the same time he was sad because his wife wouldn't see Shelley's wedding, and he wished with his whole heart that she would. She should be beside him, arranging and overseeing and fussing and adjusting and making it all right. A wedding was a woman's turf. They blossomed under its influence. They took charge. Strong had seen brutish, bullying men left cowering and speechless at weddings by small, frilly wives who grew bold and took over. He knew Shelley would handle all the arrangements, and he also knew that his wife should have been there and would have done anything to make it.

Shelley took on the extra challenge without skipping a beat. Strong signed the checks. The closer the wedding came, the more ambivalent he felt.

When the wedding was over and done, after the parties and receptions and receptions and parties, he drove home slowly and slept for two days. Then he went back to work. It was nine months since his wife had died.

◆ ◆ ◆

On the third day after the wedding, Strong stood in front of a bridal shop window in the city and realized he had paid $2,000 too much for Shelley's gown. Natalia appeared like an apparition in the reflection before him. At first he wasn't sure it was her and refused to turn and look.

She wore a dark gray suit with pearls and matching pearl earrings, and her obsidian hair was tied back with a red scarf. In the back of Strong's mind, a distant thought occurred: How do they do that every day? Men arose and kept marching forward till they got to work: Shower, shave, clothes, breakfast, train, and newspaper happened as they maintained forward motion. But these women created a work of art.

When he finally faced her, he was struck by how little he felt.

Natalia looked at him. "I wanted to be sure you were all right."

There was no awkwardness, no explanation or embarrassment. She was concerned. He appreciated that. He had been down a very long road since he last saw her, and he was a very different man. He expected he looked it, and was vain enough to ask.

"I'm surprised you recognized me," he said, indicating his all-gray hair with a bob of his head.

"It was turning, anyway," she said with a small glint in her eye.

"Really! You never told me."

"I didn't want to hurt your feelings."

"Well, you're right there, it probably would have," he replied, looking back at the wedding dress.

She took a breath. "Listen, I'm not sure how to say this, but I am so sorry. I wish it were different for you."

He kept looking in the window. "Thank you. Me, too."

They lapsed into silence, staring blindly at the expensive white gowns in front of them. Weddings, he thought. They seem so symbolic. Yes, but of what – beginning, end, both? He wasn't sure what he was feeling.

Natalia knew quite well what she felt – stupid and awkward. He wasn't making it easy. He was acting like a stranger. Perhaps she had been naïve. After all, the man had lost his wife, but she had hoped for more from a man for whom she turned herself inside out, laid herself wide open, a blank sheet for him to write on. She had thought about him day and night for so long she had ached, and now here he was and she couldn't wait to get away. How can I get out of here gracefully? she asked herself. She looked around.

"Anyway, I really am sorry, and I wish there were something I could do," she said, feeling completely at a loss. "I have got to be running. I am glad you are well. You look ... great." He was silent. Not a word. Thanks a lot!

She stumbled on. "You have been through hell, and you have come out on the other side OK, it seems. So ... take care. I hope for you the best."

She was reverting to English with Russian construction, for some stupid reason. Damn, she sounded so dumb! She put out her hand to shake good-bye and just get the hell out of there. Why was she offering her hand? She never wanted to touch him again in her life!

He turned and took it. "Thank you," he replied distantly.

She shook once, emphatically, and fled down the street as fast as she could. She felt stifled. It had been one of the most oppressive moments of her life. The last time she felt so miserable she had been a teenager with a boy in Odessa who was not particularly adept. She practically raced down the Manhattan sidewalk.

When Natalia was nearly half a block distant and almost out of earshot, a very loud voice said, "Actually, it's been sort of enlightening." She realized he must be still standing in front of the window, pondering. A few people on the sidewalk looked curiously back toward him as they marched by: Another nut talking to himself in the city.

His words found her down the block. She took several more steps and then came to a halt, despite herself. A guy behind bumped into her and said, "Shit," as he edged by.

She turned and called out, "What? Enlightening – did I hear right?" She ignored the people who looked at her like she was crazy as they tried to figure out what was going on.

"You did," he said, once again quite loud. His words almost echoed between the tall buildings.

Avoiding the stares, she approached him carefully and while still at a distance said, "Perhaps you're not all right after all. You need some rest." She almost added, "You prick."

They were ten steps apart. People gave them a wide berth, as if an explosion were imminent.

Strong turned back to the window. Finally he said, "I would like to tell you about it."

She didn't want this, if it was the last thing in the world. She had just kissed him off in her mind, freed herself of this awful burden, and now he was calling her back. Why was she listening? What in hell was she doing?

Natalia paused there and considered for quite a long time. People brushed by, irked. She came a little closer and said, "Are you in some kind of senior citizen mentor mode, or something?" She felt a small thrill when she saw he was taken aback. She had wanted to be as mean as possible, hoping to kill this off quickly and get on with her life.

"Well, yes. But it'll be worth it. Among friends," he added.

"You didn't have to say that."

"Maybe not. But I felt like saying it," he said.

That gave her pause. He seemed different, defiant. "I'm sorry. I shouldn't have been rude. You should have thrown a verbal right cross," she said.

"The thought occurred to me," he said, and smiled slightly for the first time, then turned to look at her. "From here a verbal left hook would have been better." That made her laugh. "It was a left hook, remember?"

EIGHT

JUST FRIENDS

They met two weeks later, for lunch at a café on First Avenue. The place had tables on the sidewalk and a terrace in back. It was a bright, early spring day. The sun was warm, but the air remained crisp. The shadows still held winter.

Strong was surprised with himself. He had scarcely thought about her once they had set up their lunch. In fact, he almost forgot until his secretary buzzed to remind him thirty minutes before. He jumped up from his desk, still talking on the phone, and got his coat on as he cut off a client on the other end.

Amazing. A woman he couldn't get enough of nine months before, whom he had wanted to put in his mouth and roll around on his tongue to taste every part of her like hard candy, and now he had nearly forgotten their appointment. Life was funny. He strolled in five minutes late.

She was waiting. "I'm going to slug you if you say you're sorry for being late," was the first thing out of her mouth.

"Have you ever noticed there seems to be a recurring pugilistic theme to our friendship?" he asked as he pulled out his chair to sit down.

She guffawed. "What are we going to talk about?" she inquired, regaining control.

He took a deep breath. "Life," he said, as he leaned forward across the table and put on a solemn face. Her face fell, and he burst out laughing.

"Well, I'm glad to see you're taking this none too seriously," she replied.

"You thought I was serious!" he said. "You looked so worried, believe me."

It was a beautiful day. They were on the terrace. They began to talk. He started and she let him go on and on. She could have said a thing or two, but chose not to. Apparently he needed to let all the air out, to exhale in an enormous way. He began with his wife's stumbles and falls in the kitchen, and proceeded through to the end and the way her death made him implode, dissolve, diminish into himself. He regretted, but he wasn't sorry, she noted. He seemed — what was the word? Wise. He was reflective and appreciative of his wife and all they had gone through, even her death, like not regretting a bruise.

By the end of the afternoon they were both drinking a second glass of wine.

When she felt cold she looked at her watch. She jumped up. "Do you have any idea what time it is?"

"Come to think of it, I don't," he said in surprise, looking around like an absent-minded professor.

"It is almost five."

"Oh my god, have I taken a breath in the last three hours? The last time I talked like that it was my only time on cocaine. I was brilliant. Everyone fell asleep."

"I am not asleep, but I am late," she said, rushing into her coat.

"Right. God, sorry about this. Listen, how about another coffee a week or two down the line? This has been very helpful," he said, collecting the bill.

"Of course. You don't have to ask," she said, working on her American contractions.

"I don't think I have said one single thing I had planned to relate to you. I just prattled on. For that you deserve a medal."

"Sure. Forget it. Talk to you in a week."

"Right. Thanks. Take care."

"You never have to say 'thanks' to me."

He didn't know what to make of that, and waved goodbye.

◆ ◆ ◆

A week later a gift arrived in her office. Natalia opened it. It was a large piece of chocolate with something about boxing inscribed on it. She giggled and dug in.

With perfect timing, he called. "You got it?" he asked.

Her mouth was full of chocolate, and she had a hard time enunciating. "Yeth, I god id," was the best she could do.

"It's a boxing medallion, and you're invited to the fights next Wednesday night," he said.

"The fights? God. Okay, I accept," she said through the chocolate, hunting for a napkin. It came out "akthept".

"That's a pretty bad cold you got there," he said. "You should take some chocolate for it." He hung up.

"Fuck you," she said through the chocolate to a dial tone.

♦ ♦ ♦

At the fights, Natalia felt like china in a bull shop. Everyone seemed fat and sweaty. They ate hot dogs slathered with mustard and swilled beer. The arena was smoky and hot, with steep, boney wooden seats that plunged down to the ring below. She wished she had worn slacks. She lost count of the endless preliminary bouts with young men in great shape beating the hell out of each other.

"How're you doin'?" he asked jocularly, as if the place required a different use of the language than his usual. Phony, she thought.

"Wanna a beer? Hey, two beers over here," he called to a guy in the aisle without waiting for her answer. She accepted the damp wax cup and tried to smile. The crowd roared at something, some particularly good whack, she suspected, and his attention was diverted.

She feigned interest until one young man was badly hurt and fell over. She could see it was serious. There was a look of surprise in his eyes, as if he suddenly realized how dangerous it was. Two days later she read he died of a brain hemorrhage.

She didn't watch much after that bout, but tried to get interested in the crowd. She couldn't find a single person she thought she would like, but Strong was enjoying himself immensely. His man won the final bout. When it was all over, she was glad to go home.

"You didn't enjoy that," he said in the cab to her apartment as they roared down Park, making light after light in the chill night.

"No," she said in response. "Why do you like it?" She caught a lingering smell of smoke in the cab, which she liked.

"It's honest. It's direct. Honesty – that's what I see in boxing. There's no place to hide."

He faced forward next to her. Why didn't he look at her anymore when he spoke? "I'll say. Life on the line. I thought boxing was supposed to be an art. This was brutal. They were just hitting each other. Well, I'm choosing the next bout." The smoke smell made her want a cigarette.

"No kidding? What fight?" He finally turned to look at her.

The cab came to an abrupt stop in front of her dingy apartment building. She inadvertently grabbed his arm, then quickly let go. "The ballet. Tickets on me. I'll let you know when. Good night."

"The ballet?" he asked as she got out and slammed the door shut.

◆ ◆ ◆

Several weeks later, Natalia called him to nail down the date. They hadn't spoken in the meantime.

"Uh, let me make sure I'm free," Strong said when she told him why she had called.

"You're free," she replied. He was so predictable. "I'll pick you up at your office. We'll have dinner – my treat." She wasn't going to give him any reason to weasel out.

"Uh, well, OK," he said.

She had always loved the ballet. It was beautiful, graceful, magical, and alive. At the entr'acte, he bought wine at the bar. "I need help here," he said. He was apparently trying to understand ballet. Natalia was surprised he had never made the effort before. One part of her said, What do you expect of Americans? Maybe she was still a Russian at heart.

She stood before the tall windows at Lincoln Center in a short black cocktail dress with a high collar and tight half-sleeves. She liked to wear heels and no bra. Tonight was no different. It was raining.

"You find honesty in boxing? Well, I find it in ballet – so perfect, so impossible, so wonderful. No guile. Everything on the line. Or as you would say, no place to hide."

"Well, yes – at least as far as the costumes are concerned."

She ignored the comment and left for the ladies' room. There was insouciance about her, a confidence bordering on arrogance. It caught people's attention. They looked at her retreating figure, black hair swinging, lips red and set, dark eyes. She came back the same way.

"Why are you looking at me like that?" she asked.

"I was admiring you," he said formally, bowing slightly.

"Um," she said, considering what he meant. She took his arm as they returned for the second act, for some reason feeling sad.

At the end he seemed to have enjoyed it. They stood and applauded, then made their way out. Natalia held his arm. She wanted to lean against his shoulder, but was afraid. Something held her back. He seemed distant and stiff.

At the curb Strong hailed a cab and put her into it. She swept her legs in and slipped over, waiting for him to join her, but he didn't. She looked straight ahead to mask her disappointment. She had wanted the night to continue, if nothing else to keep talking.

"So, are you seeing someone now?" he asked out of the blue, leaning down into the cab to look at her.

She sat back, then turned to look at him. What in hell was he talking about? She wasn't "seeing" anyone, goddamnit. Wasn't that pretty obvious? As a matter of fact, she sort of thought she was "seeing" him, grief and all, although now that she considered it, she had seen damn little of that. What is with this guy? What does he care about? Doesn't he miss his wife? Is he from a different planet? Does he want me?

"Do you really want to know?" she asked, and shut the door without waiting for an answer. "Let's go," she told the driver. The cab took off.

Strong watched the tail lights of the cab disappear in the mid-town traffic. Whoa, he said to himself. He wasn't sure what to think. People could be so strange. With his wife, most of the time he knew what she was thinking, even though he might not like it. He hadn't fully appreciated their intimacy until just then, watching the cab tail lights disappear.

He felt fractured, disjointed, unsure of himself. After all he'd been through, he didn't want any part of the passion this beautiful young woman could trigger. It wasn't helpful, constructive. It was confusing. He wasn't ready for it. He wanted to retain a distance, not get sucked in, keep his feet on the ground. That would be good.

At the same time he had to admit he liked her, respected her, thought she was exceptional, savvy, and yes, strikingly beautiful.

At the ballet, he had watched her move across the red-carpeted floor in her cocktail dress, and been close to the old feelings by the time she floated up to him.

She would make someone a great wife.

She was all the more appealing because she herself didn't fully understand her beauty, he felt. Oh, she knew damn well that men found her attractive, would make a pass if they could. She could control that, he was sure, like most European women, but she had no idea how strong her beauty and character really were. It is a blessing that she does not know, he thought, chortling at his failure to use a contraction in his mind. She might be tempted to take advantage of it. So he kept his mouth shut.

Strong decided to retreat for a while, so when she called he was consciously distant. "Hey, how about coffee at the end of the day?" she inquired. He had taken her call in his office following another hot dog lunch.

"Can't," he said. "Sorry. Got a meeting." He always talked cryptically when he lied.

One day, walking down the sidewalk talking to himself he realized he was actually talking to his wife, but she was gone. There would be no recapping over dinner. There would be absolutely nothing over dinner. He stared at something in a store window, taking time to recover. He had been badly beaten up. Truth be known, he was stumbling around, walking in circles and bumping into things. Later in the week, his office manager found him alone in the conference room, charts and layouts spread before him on the large table.

"What's up?" the man asked.

"All ready for our two o'clock pitch," Strong said.

"That's tomorrow," the manager replied, and closed the door. Strong sat there alone for fifteen minutes.

Natalia was a relief, a hand to hold in the mist, maybe she might become a lifelong friend, but that was it. He would return the favor, help her if he could, but there would be nothing more.

Their relationship continued its instructional air. He took her here and there and pointed out things, and she pretended to learn and appreciate what, for the most part, she already knew. He patronized her, as if she were a child. She humored him, as if he were an invalid.

"It's not by chance the Impressionists and Debussy were contemporary," he intoned one afternoon at the Frick Collection as they wandered from room to room. "They were doing the same thing, but in different media."

She took a breath and bit her tongue. She had heard precisely the same thing ten years before. It must be some strange off-shoot of grief, she surmised, and so allowed him considerably more leeway than she would have otherwise. After a while it began to piss her off.

For his part, Strong mused that she should meet someone her age, someone fine and ready and kind and upstanding and all that, someone willing to slug it out on occasion, stand toe to toe and verbally duke it out with her, no quarter given or asked, just brute intellectual force salted with a dash of passion and a splash of spit. She was good at that. She packed a hell of a wallop with her left hand, but her mouth was even better. He half-pitied and half-envied the guy. He was too old to go through all that again.

◆ ◆ ◆

Out in the country, he was adjusting to life without his wife, and it was not only lonely but also boring. The weekend dinner encounters with extra females continued. There would be the customary host greetings of, "Hi, how're you doing, glad you could come, you remember (her name)," which he didn't. He wanted to be relaxed and open, but instead he was instantly wary. There, at the edge of the living room seated primly would the "other guest for the evening". It was awful. They were all supposed to pretend this wasn't a set-up. He would act surprised and pleased, both complete lies, and the hosts and their other guest would try to be spontaneous and wasn't it all wonderful! To Strong, it felt like cocktails on the Titanic, after the iceberg.

It reminded him of blind dates at college, which for him had always been a disaster. One time a girl had marched down the dorm staircase, took one look at him, said, "Hello," shook his hand formally and didn't say another word for the entire evening except, "Good night." Thinking of it now, he admired her for being so forthright. She must have thought he was a pill — who knows, maybe he was – and she wasn't about to compromise herself with an evening of social pleasantries. Good for her!

But these nights – Jesus, he wasn't ready to do it all over again. Self-service looked like a very viable, permanent alternative. He started renting X-rated films. At least the girls were gorgeous.

Before too many months he felt awkward around the small town and began to watch out. He had a sneaking suspicion some of these women were plotting to "bump into" him at the market, the bank, or someplace. "Oh, hi! I didn't know you came here." He started shopping at odd hours, and pushed his cart along fast like no other shopper, zooming up and down the aisles and hurling stuff into it. His checkout friend caught on and laughed.

"One of the ladies inquired about you the other day," she said rolling her eyes. "Asked if you'd been around. I played dumb," she said whizzing his items through the optical scanner.

"Thank God," he replied. "I owe you one."

"Naw. You're fun talking to. Get outta here before she shows up."

He did.

By now Strong dared venture outside the frozen food department, and it felt good. He would stop to discuss the cuts of meat with the butcher in his long, blood-spattered apron, and the fresh produce with the grocer while the man sprayed the greens. He felt quite cosmopolitan, like a Parisian, he imagined, versed in the culinary arts, which he wasn't. Maybe he should affect ascots or a beret. He didn't care if he looked ridiculous. When he took a night cooking course, it might as well have been printed in the local newspaper. It became a dinner topic. To his surprise and delight, he had a knack for sauces. Part of the fun was sipping wine while stirring. He and the sauce were both reduced by half.

And then, it began to pick up. Weekday nights were still terrible, but come the weekend, all hell broke loose. Strong was definitely the primary designated target – good-looking, good company, good house, healthy, and relatively well-off. He felt like he was in the sights of just about every single woman in town aged thirty-five to sixty.

The extra women at the cocktail parties got better, and in one or two cases, younger. To his delight, cleavage came back into fashion. Skirts and dresses were also getting shorter, and slacks snugger, he was pleased to note, local trends he seemed to inspire. The heat was on, and hooks were in the water. They were attractive, but not once did he nibble the bait. He knew the price. For one thing, it would make him swim in waters he wasn't interested in broaching. For another, it would take him off the market, and all this attention was fun.

As for the women, it was a small town, and everyone knew what was what. One of his more attractive dinner partners had practically thrown herself in his arms over dinner one night. He remembered that three years before, her husband had keeled over on the golf course. She had dropped off the social radar for a while, but now she was apparently trying to make a comeback. She certainly had the means – a huge bank account and a body that was only slightly frayed at the edges. Over the soup she had looked at Strong like it had been one hell of a long time since she had had a man, and she was confident he could do the job. Two more drinks and he was afraid she would spread herself across the table for dessert. By her third cocktail she damn near did. She made it clear her number was in the phone book. Strong fled before coffee, and never called. Later he had seen her once in the village and she had crossed the street.

◆ ◆ ◆

For her part, Natalia got up each morning, went to work, went home and watched the phone. What the hell was going on?

When it rang, she sat on her fingers for three rings, then removed her earring and answered as casually as possible. It was never him. About the second glass of wine, she would go next door and bum a cigarette from the artist who lived there and was always happy to oblige a fellow sinner. When Strong finally called, she pretended to be distracted.

"Hello? Yes?" she asked, recognizing his voice immediately and fiddling with something, anything.

"There is a wonderful Kandinsky retrospective at MOMA. We should go. You should see it. Do you know Kandinsky?"

She almost laughed. Her thesis in her last year at college had been on Kandinsky and his influence on Jungian psychology. She knew more about Kandinsky than this jerk would learn in three lifetimes. "Kandinsky? No, I don't think so," she replied. "Take someone else." She could tell that stirred his pot.

Walking the Village streets on the weekend to get a handle on her thoughts, she saw it was stupid to recall their early days when she was drunk with him day and night, wrong though it was, wrong for him and wrong for her. But she would never regret the exclamations he had elicited, the cries, the sudden tears. He had squeezed her heart, and life spurted out. How could she forget that?

On the other hand, this new relationship was entirely different. He was avuncular, which made her feel – what? Clumsy, incapable, unfeminine. Gone was any pretense at romance. She knew being realistic was all for the best, but she still didn't like it. Romance might be a lot of things including stupid, but romance was a hell of a lot of fun.

She felt as if she had jumped from the second story and landed firmly with both feet on solid ground – blam! There were no illusions down here. Life was mundane and largely boring, with only minor victories such as stumbling onto a sale at Bloomingdale's or landing a new client. There wasn't any soaring. She couldn't get off the ground, try as she might. She was down to earth, and earthbound wasn't what she hoped and yearned for.

After a month of only two phone calls and no face-to-face visits, her steam started to rise. She got a tight-lipped look. People avoided her at the office. Her heels made a lot of noise coming down the hall. When she noticed one guy fleeing into the men's room, she realized she had gone too far. The time had arrived to do something about her frustrations. She was determined to find out what was what with this Benno Strong guy who, for the last few months, had treated her like a cross between an old college chum and a kid sister.

She also wanted to know what was what with her. Honestly, she didn't know. She had been in love with him; there was no denying that, and now she was ... something else. There wasn't a name for it. Hollywood didn't do stories on people betwixt and between. She couldn't think of anything in Tolstoy, either.

Perhaps she was just curious. At the edges of her heart she remembered clinging to him like there was no tomorrow, wrapped around him like a wet towel. The thought could still make her thrill for a moment, but the moment quickly evaporated.

Then there had been the long silence while Strong wrestled with unknown devils as his wife lost her grip on life. When Natalia heard from his office that the woman was dying, she had put down the phone and burst into tears. She didn't know why. Was she crying for him? Was it for his wife? For herself? All of them? God, who knew?

How she had ached during those months! There were times when she had clung to her pillow and cried through the night. When she awoke in the morning, it was still damp, and she still clutched it. She had never been so unhappy. Some days she had gone to work like a zombie and waited for the phone to ring, hoping for someone to say something, to hear something from him, about him, but she didn't want to ask. It was someone else's life, she shouldn't be a part of it, and yet that was all she wanted to know day and night, night and day. Now she was trying to appreciate all this concern and thoughtfulness and patron-age crap, but she needed something more than a mentor and a surrogate dad – a lot more. She wanted a man – the smells, the feels, the fun, the fights, the taste, the life – the whole of it. Goddamnit, there was something special between men and women, something indescribable and wonderful and infuriating and funny. There was only so much she could do on her own. She needed a spark to light the fire. She found herself surreptitiously looking at men walking down the street, on the job, over a drink with friends. Was there someone out there holding a torch to set her ablaze? Was it Strong? More and more men were looking better and better. Was it another man? And then one day she met one.

NINE

LIFE IN THE COUNTRY

"Ben, come in, you look great!"

Strong's immediate neighbor to the left, a nice guy 15 years older and now retired from the import/export business, plus his truculent wife had invited him for lunch. They were an odd couple in Strong's view, completely opposite, and Strong had no idea why he liked them. The husband, with his quick smile and sparkly eyes, was forever positive and ebullient. His wife, whose pursed mouth looked like she constantly sucked on lemons, was equally negative and terse, as if to counterbalance her husband's enthusiasm and ensure the universe stayed on an even keel – not too much plus or minus. She was one of the few people Strong knew who could make a comforting statement sound awful.

"I hope you are alright," she had said to him a month after the funeral. "People in your predicament usually jump off a bridge." Strong actually laughed at that. It was the first time in a long while someone had actually been frank, so he appreciated her.

So here he was on a warm, humid New England afternoon tinged with the smell of cut grass that he loved so much. It could be a happy smell or a sad one, uplifting or smothering. Strong wasn't sure which it was as he stood at the front door of the big white house with green shutters and a brass light over the front porch. Bugs buzzed his head and he swatted them away. His neighbors were among the few people in the small town he felt he could be forthright with, so on the phone he had been.

"I'd love to come," he had said at their invitation. "Just warn me if I am going to be paired up."

"Well, I have a great friend who is coming. You probably won't like her," the wife said over the phone. She mentioned a name Strong didn't catch.

"Don't pay any attention to her," her husband had jumped in. "I don't believe you will mind your luncheon partner one tiny bit."

"OK," Strong relented.

"And don't bring a bottle of cheap wine," the wife said. "This lady will know the difference."

"Ben wouldn't bring cheap wine. He's too much a gentleman," the husband scolded. Strong laughed and hung up.

So here he was, standing in the heat at the big front door, no paired lady in sight, looking warily around. A green Jaguar sedan glistened in the driveway.

The man's wife showed up in the foyer and ushered him through the screen door carefully cradling his damn good, damned expensive bottle of Chablis Calvet. He was hoping for something light for lunch. He snuck a quick look around. No one was poised in the living room.

"Drink?"

"You bet," Strong said, relinquishing the chilled wine, eyes darting.

"I'll get it for you. Red wine, martini, scotch…?"

"Red wine will be fine, thanks." He looked forward to a quick, quiet lunch. Maybe she hadn't come.

"Fine. Help yourself to some hors d'oeuvres," the wife said. "There's actually some caviar there. We splurged, I don't know why."

"OK!" Strong said, and laughed at the unintended insult. He clapped his hands, rubbed them together and headed for the coffee table between the chintz-covered couches by the fireplace. Strong popped one of the canapés into his mouth and stood looking down considering his next target.

"I know you," a deep, female voice said behind him. It made him jump, and he turned, but not too quickly.

"You do?" Across the room was a russet-haired woman about his age. Even 20 feet away he could see she was wearing emeralds the size of a fingernail at her ears, with a bigger brooch to match nestled between her high breasts. She had thick lips, which were painted dark and smiling pleasantly, her head tipped back as if expectant.

She was casually dressed in a man's starched white dress shirt; sleeves rolled up at the cuffs, and fitted jeans, with high, expensive buff-leather heels. Casual clothes, elegant shoes – very European. Perhaps he should have worn that new blue cotton pinpoint after all.

"You don't remember …" It was a statement. He didn't, but he couldn't imagine how.

"No, but don't tell me. Let me think a minute. This could be fun. Hey," he called out to the kitchen, "make that a martini."

The lunch was fun. It turned out she had been toying with him, that they had only met once briefly years ago, but it was true, she did know him. Her husband had been one of Strong's early clients, the founder of a finance company that became a very hot property and was bought out by a Fortune 500 insurance firm. The man had died at 45 of a heart attack, very rich and very suddenly. She said he had talked glowingly of Strong's performance when he pitched the company's business early on. He credited Strong's print ad campaign with boosting the selling price by $25 million. She repeated all this to Strong over dinner. Miranda Marcuzzi was her name. Strong glowed.

"So, now, your wife. I heard all about that." This from out of the blue, before dessert. Strong wasn't sure whether he was pissed or pleased. His hosts both grabbed plates and headed for the kitchen.

"You did?"

"Yes. Have you decided what you are going to do now?"

Goddamn, this woman was direct.

"Not exactly. I wanted to step off the edge of the earth for a while, but my daughter gave me a swift kick in the butt and got me out of that."

"Good for her." They didn't dwell on the subject after that. To Strong's surprise, Miranda left early, before he had a chance to flee, and gave him a perfunctory, one-pump, no-look-back handshake. She hadn't said a word about her phone number. That was a first. Wending his way home he was surprised he didn't try to view this woman through his wife's eyes. He could only see her through his own. He felt bad. Twenty-plus years with a lover, friend, cohort, a life-partner as she had said, and you could cast them off in a few months. He felt bad.

◆ ◆ ◆

Three weeks later he got an embossed invitation to some regatta, a little blue pennant with a tiny gold star on the white card with raised border. What was this? His wife had been the sailor. He threw it in the trash in the kitchen.

Checking his messages, he heard a distinctive alto. "Yes, it's me, Miranda Marcuzzi, don't throw the invitation to the regatta away since the caviar will be superb this time – it's mine, so I should know – and if you get seasick, you don't have to go out on the water. Call if you have any questions." She left her number.

Guts, he said to himself, balls, and laughed, retrieved the invitation and called. She picked up on the second ring. There was a feminine rustle, as if she were detaching one of those huge emeralds from her ear, then, "Hello?"

"Ben Strong. How much can I eat? Caviar …"

"You have to be genteel."

"God, I don't know … "

"I'll let you know if you step over the line."

"I'm sure you will." After a little more bantering, he said, "See you there. Thanks for thinking of me."

"My pleasure," she said and hung up.

She was attractive, independent, no pushover for sure. The word "elegant" came to mind. He liked that. And perhaps she could help him forget his young Russian, far too young for him. Miranda could be a panacea for his ills. This was good.

He buried his nose in work at the office. His resolve to break with the past broke only once when late one afternoon he went to a French restaurant on Third Avenue he knew Natalia liked. It was the kind of place where the waiters acted as if they had never seen you before, even if it was dinner and you were just there for lunch. He walked in out of the rain and stood at the small bar. Ordering, he stared straight ahead, his long raincoat dripping on the black and white marble floor while he tried not to look in the mirror. Finally he gave in and glanced around. She wasn't there. He tossed down his wine and left. Going home on the train he fell asleep, almost missed his stop and had cold cuts for dinner.

The day of the regatta arrived, clear and beautiful. What should he wear? What was "proper"? He put on a blue blazer and made a face in the mirror, it looked so pretentious: Commodore Strong, ahoy. He was damned if he was going to wear a blazer to a regatta. Next he would affect a pipe. To hell with it. Just be yourself. Hadn't he learned anything in his umpteen years? He doffed the blazer, found some slacks in the back of his closet, a light blue dress shirt and a black sweater he carried in case it got cool.

Strong pulled in to the club where the regatta was being held, the gravel crunching beneath his wheels. He had never been there before. His wife and he had joined a beach club because she could work the real estate angle, write it off and have the odd lunch on the terrace. He went there about twice. There was a dinner dance every summer. No one could dance very well, himself included. He suspected the other members thought he was a jerk. They were probably right.

He parked his Saab and walked in. Everyone was gray – hair, skin, eyes – and at least 15 years his senior. He didn't know a soul except Miranda, who rescued him the moment she saw him. "Pretty grim, eh?" she said, reading his thoughts. "The young ones are all out on the water."

"How do we get out there?"

She ignored the question. "Try the caviar."

She was right. It was superb. He discovered some exotic vodka and took to downing shots, standing over the black mounds of caviar that no one else seemed to appreciate. At the third spoonful he suddenly thought of Natalia. Time was, anything Russian would have stopped his heart cold for a beat or two. Now he had a three-minute delay, proof positive that he was getting over her after all. He raised his shot glass and said, "Cheers," out loud. Some of the gray people turned. Miranda looked and smiled. What a nice lady. He waved. She laughed and waved back. He suspected he was a little high.

After 30 minutes Strong wanted to flee but couldn't, to be polite. Miranda was occupied in some official hostess capacity and didn't seem to mind his solitary vigil by the food and drink. She <u>was</u> a nice lady. The regatta was incredibly boring. There were sailboats out on the water going this way and that, then the occasional horn, once a cannon fired, and all the gray people applauded. Strong had no idea why. Thanks to the vodka, he didn't care. As to Miranda, she had invited him, so clearly the ball was in his court now, and the next move would have to be his. What would be fitting? It had to be something nice but not too nice. Go slowly.

TEN

BART

"Who are you?" a man's voice asked behind her. Natalia stood musing in front of a red and black blob painting, a style that had been *de rigeur* since the late '50s at avant-garde art galleries throughout the city. This one was in SoHo, at yet another new artist's reception. The wine was thin and the cheese stale. When she turned to look, she took a breath.

"Natalia Tsukarova," she answered, and offered her hand.

His name was Barton Bartholomew Gray, and the name fit like a Brioni suit. He was tall with dark, wavy hair and an openly friendly air. He worked for one of the big art auction houses.

After a few minutes' conversation, she had inadvertently brushed him with her hip. He laughed and said,

"Nice try. Doesn't work on me." Bart never bothered to play the straight game. Gay seemed to a part of him, but not all of him, unlike some others she had encountered.

From that first evening, things blossomed. The guy was not just good-looking, he was gorgeous, but an aristocrat with plebian tastes. He was comfortable anywhere, which made him wonderful company. He was also damned funny. They dined, they danced, they laughed, they walked and talked. She needed a friend. So did he.

Then they played tennis. Bart had powerful tan legs in cream shorts and wore a deep blue shirt that set off his dark hair. He controlled the ball beautifully, playing out each point to make it last, good to the very last stroke. It made her wonder about sex – would he do the same? She shook her head – Good Lord, what was she thinking? It had been too long.

He had a way of raising her skills, making her better than she was, hitting the ball just within her range again and again until she stretched and stretched and arched and suddenly slammed one home better than they both expected. She saw how really good he was, how well he played, getting to the ball and hitting it as if it were an extension of him, the sweep of his arm following through in a beautiful, clean arc completed by a wonderful "thwock" as the ball hit the sweet spot and flew flat out across the net just beyond her reach.

Sometimes she won the point, most times she lost, but watching Bart she didn't care. Tennis seemed to be an escape for him, a way of leaving the rest of the world behind. For her it was a way of seeing into him, piercing his defenses to catch him where he lived. When he played, he was completely focused. There was nothing else for the moment, not the slightest artifice. Natalia liked what she saw.

"You're humoring me," she said after their first match, which he won carefully.

"Only a little," he replied.

Each time they played it was the same. She went to a new level, higher and higher and she loved it. He made the sweat break out under her breasts, beneath her arms and between her legs. She pushed him hard, made him run, made him reach, made him stretch. She got better and better. He played harder and harder. His focus narrowed to a pinpoint. There was only the two of them, the ball and the net. He didn't talk much, which was fine with her.

After their fifth match – Bart had won but it took four sets – he came up to her very close and looked her square in the face. "You're getting good," he said. She glowed.

"You're making me good," she said. "What's bothering you?"

"Can't hide anything from you," he said. She had no idea what that had to do with tennis. "It's at this point that it becomes difficult for me to have women friends."

"Oh Jesus, give me a break," Natalia said. They were on the street following a shower, each with damp hair, hers blowing in the wind sweeping down the concrete canyon.

She knew what he meant, and she thought it absurd. She was getting close, and he was getting confused. She ruffled his feathers. She didn't think of him as gay, but in fact she didn't care. She just liked him. She couldn't imagine him tangled up with another man. The thought of it made her burst out laughing. Things didn't fit.

"What are you laughing at?" he asked, offended to be left out of the joke.

"Some day I'll tell you, but not right now," she said, and exploded in laughter again.

"Well, I'm glad you're having fun," he said.

"Don't worry, you'll be having fun soon, too," she said, not really knowing what she meant.

◆ ◆ ◆

A few days later, Strong called. "Hey, how are you?"
"Fine," she replied.

"OK, well, how about …" and he proposed another exhibition, apparently the next in his series of lectures to instruct her in the ways of the world.

To hell with this. "Busy, can't, gotta run, 'bye," she said in a single breath and hung up before he could say word one.

In his office, Strong realized he probably shouldn't have called in the first place. He walked around his desk for a few minutes, hands in his pockets, and promised himself not to call her for a month. At the end of that month, he would try to forgo another month. It was like quitting smoking: Take one step at a time. Never think too far in advance.

When Bart called Natalia, he was solemn, serious, as if they had come to a river they could never cross. Natalia picked up the phone and heard him take a deep breath and say, "Hello."

"Oh, get off it," she came back instantly, and laughed. She was having a great day. She had practically hung up on Strong, the sun was streaming through the windows of her skyscraper office, the river glistened in a silver sheet far below, and life was pretty damned good. She wasn't going to let Bart blow it for her. "You sound like someone just died."

"As a matter of fact," he started out, and she cut him off quick.

"Don't take yourself so goddamn seriously. There's a lot more to life than you know, so relax and enjoy it. Lunch in an hour at ..." and she named a popular place. "Be there," she said and hung up.

In fact, like the country he lived in, Bart was confused about sex. He couldn't get it right, try as he might. Early on, in high school, there had been plenty of girls but they didn't do much for him. He went through all the motions, hung out with a clique, dated a little. He liked kissing, and a full sweater still pulled him up short, but once he got in the heat of battle it seemed to be all struggle and sweat and not much else. He wanted violins in the orchestra instead of grunts in the balcony.

He didn't connect with any of the girls. They weren't sexy to him. There was no raw passion, the kind he hoped for that would make them do uncontrollable things like scream or tremble like a leaf in the wind despite themselves – just really let it rip. These girls were under control, with one eye open while they smacked, groped and ground away, trying to do it right and not get caught at the same time. He wasn't sure they were even enjoying it. He felt like they were just going through the motions. That made him feel impotent.

After a while he gave up. There were plenty of other things to do. Why embarrass yourself? He had an artistic side he was surprised to discover, since he came from a meat, potatoes and cocktails kind of family. No one played the stereo except for parties.

He went into New York and ambled around art galleries, first uptown and later down, affecting a scarf around his neck and over one shoulder, which his mother didn't like. He wasn't sure why art appealed to him so much. He liked the visual stuff, the colors, the forms, but there was something more. Perhaps it was the life style he suspected was behind all this, an indifference to most things, a passion for a few, the artists' absorption with what they were doing, to the exclusion of practically all else, including what they had.

That's what he yearned for – total immersion. How he would love to find something that drew him inexorably in so that nothing else mattered! He took to smoking Gauloise on these trips. His mother sniffed and almost said something twice when he came home, but held her tongue. He was a closet Bohemian. She could understand that. She wasn't born yesterday.

His sorties made him feel alive. In the city he felt different, reborn, detached from his proper, privileged upbringing. Later he would appreciate all his family did for him, but not now. Now he wanted something else.

When they went to Europe one summer Bart was entranced by the history that surrounded him, and by the art in fountains and buildings and churches and streets. It was everywhere. He didn't have to hunt it down like at home. And the women were different too. He saw one riding a bicycle down the street with her skirt blown up around her thighs, and she didn't try to push it down, she just kept riding, legs flashing, churning. Men looked and smiled but didn't gawk. She seemed to enjoy it. He certainly did.

In Venice, he was feeding the pigeons in a fabulous piazza when a tall German girl came up and said, "Hello?" with a question mark. She wasn't sure he spoke English.

No female stranger at home, much less a pretty one, had ever walked up to him and said, "Hello", with or without the question mark. An enormous grin spread across his face, a foolish grin he felt sure, one that would drive her away, but no, she stayed. He was thrilled. This was too good to be true. It could only be heaven where a blond with a quite tight shirt and a damn fine figure walked up to you out of the blue, said, "Hello" and stayed. He never wanted to go home.

It was natural to go to a café for an espresso or wine, so they did. Why did it never happen like this at home? There it was always so labored, so complicated, so hard. You had to make a date, set a time, think of a place. Here it was easy. Shit, who cared? He felt giddy and he hadn't even had a glass of wine. She sat across from him in the sun, her ash blond hair sparkling, and told him in that wonderful accent she was a student touring with friends, she had thought he might be an American and she wanted to practice her English. Did he mind?

Mind? Mind looking at this Aryan goddess with the cream skin, this window on another world, this ticket out of his American tour of the Continent with his parents — mind? Not on his sweet life.

He asked her to dinner, trying to figure out in the back of his mind how he could ditch his parents, meet the girl and keep the one from meeting the other. He didn't think it would be a good mix. She was staying at a student hostel, exactly what he thought he would have liked to do. Later he did and hated the thin mattresses and the communal showers. He, on the other hand, was at the Royal Danieli, a four-star establishment where a tie was expected, even in the lobby.

They met at a sort of Italian bodega filled with students, smoke, cheap wine but good food. He had a wonderful time, and even spoke some French after his third glass. The German girl – her name was Gudrun – sat next to him but spent a great deal of time talking to everyone else. He lost hope so he had another glass and focused, as much as possible, on a mousy little Italian girl who spoke French with a surprisingly bright smile and a wit to match. Just when he was getting into it, the French flowing freely, Gudrun took him by the arm and led him out. By this time he was drunk and had no idea where he was going, and didn't in the slightest care. She hailed a taxi, the regular kind not the Venice romantic gondola which would have assuredly made him throw up, and took him to bed.

There were only one or two things Bart remembered about that night clearly, but one was her shedding her clothes in the harsh fluorescent light in a white tiled bathroom, and the other was the assured way she took him in hand and brought him confidently to life. He had absolutely no fear or apprehension. They fell into bed laughing, awkward because he was drunk, but still he found home, filled it and made her sigh and then moan in delight and appreciation. He enjoyed himself immensely. She seemed as satisfied as he was, though he had absolutely no idea what she was saying in the heat of passion since it was all in German. The next morning he couldn't figure out if he was happier about the sex or the fact that he had done something adventurous and European. His mother gave him a look when he returned to the hotel. His father had a small grin and didn't say anything.

He returned to America a different person, somewhat to his family's regret. Europe was a learning experience, but nothing was supposed to change. Bart had. He went to one formal dance at his mother's urging — black tie with girls chattering in awkward strapless dresses — and it seemed so pointless. One cute girl had tried to be nice and had asked him to dance. He had said to her matter-of-factly, "I don't think so." So much for girls. He began looking for friendship, and that was more forthcoming with males.

When one of these young men introduced him to same-sex sex, it wasn't the shock Bart thought it would be — Okay, that feels good, whoa, how about that! — and from then on he went along out of habit. At least it wasn't as irksome and awkward as with the girls, who were so strange and smothering.

But all in all, now his life was pretty sexless. He still found himself admiring women. They were so unique, this one especially, this Natalia. But he considered himself gay, mostly.

In his mind's eye Bart had carved an image that he wanted to fit. After all, there was no doubt in the world that just about every gay guy he knew had more taste and style than his straight peer, black guys especially. They could put clothes together in such a way he had to look two or three times. His gay friends knew food and art and opera, even ballet. They could converse, really talk, communicate. Being gay cut through the social chatter, the status talk, and the is-his-job-better-than-mine, is-she-doing-better-than-I-am stuff. It set him apart, marked him. Being gay was a stigma, an adversity, a difference like being black, but it was good, he found. There was a kind of unity in it. It brought him together with others who felt the same way. It eliminated the supercilious, awful "I did this and then met so-and-so" kind of conversation that guaranteed he would run out of something to say once he exhausted his list of funny stories and interesting events. Bart hated conversations like that, most of all when he found himself doing them. He liked people who talked about what they thought and felt, not what they owned and where they had gone. If they didn't have anything to say, they shut up. He could eat dinner in a dingy apartment with friends who were a taxi driver and short order cook and have a wonderful time. It was as if being gay kept them on their toes – he laughed at that one – and made them think about the world around them. That was what he liked about being gay – it put him outside the mainstream and into a separate world where being good and knowledgeable and appreciative and sensitive – he winced at the word – was all that mattered. Because he was gay, he was a renegade, a maverick. Being gay was the great equalizer. He loved the freedom. He wouldn't give it up for anything.

On the flip side, Bart had a deathly fear of being ordinary, plain, a shoe salesman in later life. Even that had been turned on its ear when he met a sweet Latino guy selling shoes in Saks who was so good, so clear, so perceptive and so tasteful that he made shoes seem like a work of art, a wonder to behold and a privilege to wear. Bart bought three pairs. That's what he wanted from being gay – to enjoy whatever he was doing and not be pegged by class or status or religion or race, but just by, by … what … by balls! That made him laugh right out loud.

And now Natalia was getting comfortable and close and that was not what he wanted. It didn't fit. He wasn't going to get involved with a woman. It would shatter his whole way of looking at himself, his way of living. And she was laughing!

They met, as agreed, for lunch. He was reticent. She was buoyant. He pouted, she teased. Eventually she won him over. They were both in stitches by the end of the meal, saying to hell with their jobs for the rest of the day, let's just tour the Village.

So they did. Arm in arm they watched the Village unfold – chess games in the park, homeless snoozing on stoops, vendors hawking questionable goods on the street corners. She bought him a large T-shirt that said, "Gay is Good!". He took it back and got an extra-small that said, "Bigger is Better". Finally they ended up in her apartment.

Natalia hadn't thought a thing about it until he was in the door and looking awkward. She said, "Oh come on in, for Pete's sake. What would you like – some tea?" She didn't want to imply anything with wine or beer.

"Tea? Tea? Do I look like some poof, for Chrissakes?" he exploded. "I want a beer at the very least!"

"Yo, jeez, OK, no problem, Rockie," she said in a deep voice and swaggered into the kitchen to fill the order.

"And put on the T-shirt," he called after her.

"Yo, OK, OK," was the reply. There was the rustle of paper, the doffing of clothes and the donning of them. She came back with two beers, two glasses and a very tight T-shirt. He burst out laughing.

"It says 'Bigger is Better'," he sputtered, pointing at her chest, "but you're not …"

"I know, I know. Don't rub it in," she replied, crossing her arms, glancing furtively down at her small, taught chest.

"No, no, it's OK, they're fine, I mean you're fine. Oh shit, look, you've got great tits! That didn't come out exactly the way I meant it to," he said and took a long swig.

"Have we finished with my equipment?"

"I think so," was his reply. "Don't cross your arms."

She had a lovely evening, heating leftovers and chugging beer, and he seemed to be enjoying himself aplenty, too. She pulled out her Puccini, which elicited a confession from him that *Madama Butterfly* was the first opera he truly loved. He told her about growing up on Long Island where everyone was a progressive Democrat and he was a closet Republican. "I've always been in the closet about something," he said with a laugh.

"Oh, shit, everyone has secrets. Don't worry about it. One day I may tell you mine," she said.

"About 'him'?"

She got up and started to pace. "I don't know if I can talk about it right now," she replied.

"Sorry. I shouldn't have brought it up."

"No, no, it's all right. Well, maybe you shouldn't have, but here goes," and she launched into the tale of meeting Strong, being wary of him, afraid of him right from the beginning, even before their initial bout.

"I slapped him square in the face. You should have heard it, it sounded like a gunshot."

"You <u>what</u>?"

She tapped him on the cheek in demonstration, then settled back into the couch to continue her monologue. She described, sitting in shadow, what she had felt.

As the words tumbled out, she realized that she had been instinctively afraid not for anything Strong did or was but because of what she felt, an almost feral pull toward a man whom she instantly admired and liked but who was all wrong, wrong for her, wrong for him, wrong for everything. Strong thought he had it under control but he didn't, she said. To her surprise, neither did she. It was as if they had fallen in a river and the river had swept them away, try to swim as they might. They were foolish.

She admitted she had never been so overwhelmed by anyone in her life, and then she told Bart about Strong's wife, her suddenly becoming ill and fading fast until in a matter of weeks she was gone. Bart seemed to be at a loss as to what to say.

"I didn't know what to think," she continued. "Did I bring this on him? On her? What was my part?" she asked rhetorically, walking in circles on the small prayer rug.

"Don't be ridiculous. Of course not. Don't beat yourself up about this," he said.

"Don't beat myself up? What does that mean – stop looking at it honestly? Hey, I'm just seeing what happened and trying to figure out what I'm responsible for!" Natalia said.

"Well, you're not responsible for everything."

"Oh, yeah? Let me ask you something. Do you think there is some vengeful force in the universe that makes sure you don't get away with anything, and when you make a mistake, puts it right back in your face? Is there? I've always thought so." Bart didn't say anything.

"Did you ever feel that if your life was too good, too blessed," she continued, not looking at him now, "that God or whatever would come along and knock you off your feet, pull the carpet out sorta like, 'Not so fast, buster, you haven't got it all down pat. Try this one on for size!' and leave you holding a handful of shit?" She punctuated this with a stomp of her foot.

"I always suspected that, when I was a kid," she continued. "I remember at gymnastics camp one day – don't laugh, goddamnit, I had won a state scholarship, and this was Russia – I fell down some stairs and broke my arm. That was the end of gymnastics for me. I started looking over my shoulder after that. I think I was on to something. Later I realized that was my first religious thought.

"And you, Mr. Beautiful, Mr. Gorgeous – oh, he's blushing!" – by now she was feeling the beer they had been drinking for two hours – "you grow up in Never-Never Land here in America where the sun always shines, the boats always sail and the money never stops – 'Isn't life just grand?'" – she did a twirl – "and one day you get a nice neat package in the mail that you open and it says, 'Hey, dude, you're gay! Fag City!'"

He winced on the couch. She considered reining in, then blundered on, the beer doing its work on her tongue.

"Did you start to wonder about that, about how the world works, that maybe it wasn't all so grand and sweet, and maybe God – whatever – wasn't really 'good people', as they say here, but something of a prick? 'Cause frankly I think that's a bit of a burden, the gay thing, if you want to know the truth. I wouldn't want it, I can tell you that, open-mindedness and all that stuff aside. I'm confused enough without having to sort through my sexual prefer-ences every time I meet someone new."

She could see she was opening doors he had closed a long time ago, and that he wasn't sure he wanted her to take a look inside.

She plowed on. "Well, I sure as hell wish it weren't so, I can tell you, this gay thing for you, because I think you're damned attractive, damned good looking, and would make a hell of a good roll in the hay as you Americans say, is what I think!"

Bart was silent. She couldn't read his expression. She plucked at her shirt.

"That's right, small tits and all. Does that shock you? You want to run out the door? Do you? Fuck! Did I do this to us all — to him, to me, to his wife, and now to you? Did I? Stop staring at me! Tell me what you think! Goddamnit, give me an answer! I feel so awful! So ... responsible!" She fell onto the couch, put her hand to her mouth and began to cry silently.

She felt him put his arms around her when she started to crumble and shake. She wet his shirt. At long last she stopped and took a few deep breaths.

"Well, I'll bet you're glad you came for dinner," she said.

"Actually, I am. But you certainly have upset my apple cart."

"Oh great, just what I intended to do."

A bit later he left, giving her a kiss on the brow. "No crying about this all night," he instructed.

"Right," she said. "Thanks." She kissed him lightly on the lips and held on. Sniff. She noticed that he didn't push her away.

◆ ◆ ◆

One afternoon, on the way to their tennis game, she spotted Bart across First Avenue and waved.

"You look gorgeous," he called as loudly as he could, a great grin on his face.

"Can't hear you," she said, not believing she heard him right, hoping she had, and darting into the traffic.

A Yellow cab going twenty hit her full force on her left side. Later she said, "All I remember is a bang and then the world went upside down." It had. She flipped up in the air and did a full somersault before coming down flat on her back on the pavement. Sports gear spilled out of her bag and slithered across the pavement. A truck ran over her racket. The cabbie, a fellow Russian, had jammed on the brakes at impact and the traffic behind followed suit.

Bart had watched it all in slow-motion horror, screaming as he ran across the street, nearly getting hit himself, to crouch over her, tears pouring down his cheeks, please, please, Natalia, hear me, speak to me, Nat-Nat-Nat. Her eyelids had fluttered so he knew she was at least alive.

◆ ◆ ◆

When she awoke in the hospital a day later he was seated in the chair in the corner of her room. There was a light over his shoulder, it was dark out. He had fallen asleep reading.

"Hey," she said in a whisper.

He jumped out of his seat and darted over. "Oh my God, you're there!"

"Of course I'm here. I'm not sure how much of me is here." She suspected she was thoroughly drugged because nothing hurt at all. "Prognosis, doctor."

"Bunch of broken stuff, nothing permanent, lots of drugs."

"That's not so bad. The drugs are pretty good."

"I bet." He kissed her forehead.

Then it got worse. They were talking two days after the accident, she propped up in the pillows, trying to itch her leg in its cast, when her head rolled around like it was coming off her neck. Bart laughed, then rushed out for a nurse when she didn't come around. The nurse took one look and called out, "Code Blue." Bart had no idea what that meant, but clearly it wasn't good. He began to pray, which he hadn't done for a very long time.

Two doctors arrived who looked like they had just graduated high school. They went right to work with tubes, injections and insertions. Bart tried to make sense out of what they were saying, but it was no use. One good thing was that her heart was beating strong, that much he understood, but nothing else seemed to work right. One doc would ask a question and then someone would say, "No response," or "Negative," or something else awful. When they finally noticed him they ordered him out of the room. A nurse directed him to the cafeteria, where he sat in the florescent glare with a cup of coffee, surprisingly strong, for three hours.

Try as he might, he couldn't focus on a single thing but the dull ache in his stomach, a kind of negative weight that pulled him down like gravity through a very dark hole. At one point he got up to call his mother, who listened gravely and offered to come into the city to be with him. He declined.

He knew he should call Strong, of course, but he didn't. He suspected Natalia wouldn't want him to, and he had no desire to share her with anyone else, particularly a man he had never met, so he didn't. Instead he nursed his anguish, his fears, like an open wound. If it looked like she was going to die, he would call, but he refused to believe that. He really didn't know what to believe anymore.

And now Natalia was, was what? So important to him, nearly his whole world, if the truth be known. He would do anything for her, and practically had. If she had needed a kidney he would have stripped off his shirt and walked right into the operating room without a pause. Natalia shattered his whole way of looking at himself, his way of living. What should he do?

◆ ◆ ◆

Over the next six weeks, while she lay unconscious and any future seemed pointless, he changed. He became more grave — that was the only way he could describe it. His mother had used the word, and his mother was right. Life became serious, no longer a game, a practice run, tennis match, but the real thing. He walked the city streets in straight lines with his jaw set, not weaving in and out to window shop, to gawk at this guy or that girl. Several of his gayer friends, the ones who worked hard at it, seemed no longer fun but absurd. They turned on him, slashing and mocking his new gravity. He didn't care.

One afternoon his pager went off. He was standing at a urinal *in flagrante delicto* when they damned thing started to chirp and vibrate. Cursing, he ripped it off his waist and looked at the number, trying not to make a mess. The hospital. He found a phone and called.

"What is it, is she OK, why did you call, what's up, tell me!"

"It's good news. She just came around."

He jumped in a cab and was there in 20 minutes, despite the rush hour traffic. He had to run the last five blocks because of traffic, so he was dripping when he piled into her room.

"Nat, I am so glad … " he began, then burst into tears. She was barely conscious, but she heard him and made a tiny motion with her hand. He held onto it and tried to calm down. After ten minutes, one of the surfer doctors tapped him on the shoulder.

"Could I speak with you?" he asked. Without waiting for an answer, he turned and left the room. Outside, in the corridor holding a clipboard and seeming to have a hard time looking at Bart, he said, "We suspect she can't talk."

"What?"

"There appears to have been some kind of stroke subsequent to the accident, and it has affected her ability to speak."

Bart sat down heavily in a plastic chair, trying to stifle his joy at her recovery, which now had to be tempered with — what? This wasn't fair. There was no way to know how to react.

She cried at first, of course, when she realized she had something to say but couldn't say it. He saw the shock in her eyes. She later described it: she would open her mouth but the words stopped at the back of her teeth and nothing came out. This for a woman who had had a very fast lip, which now lay idle, on hold. After the initial shock for both of them, she got a gritty, pissed look and started writing notes furiously. Before long that seemed good enough to him, but apparently not to her. "MUST TALK!" she wrote when he had suggested she was doing just fine.

"OK, so let's practice."

"Not with you," she indicated with a waved finger, and sent him out of the room. Her therapist explained: she was too embarrassed by the sounds she was making to let him hear. It took two weeks before she could say "yes" and "no" clearly. Oddly enough, she did considerably better in Russian. She was thrilled with her improvement, and he celebrated with a bottle of smuggled champagne. By then she was sitting up and tooling around in a wheelchair, broken leg thrust out before her like a plaster lance.

"I don't know about this therapy business," he said, pouring her a second glass, eye on the door lest a nurse barge in and confiscate.

"No?"

"No. This way may be the best of all worlds. I can say anything, and you can't talk back."

She rolled over and whacked him on the shoulder.

◆ ◆ ◆

Six weeks in bed were followed by three months of therapy – with mixed results. Natalia could speak, say just about anything, but it was slow going except for short words. She never called Strong for obvious reasons: she couldn't talk well, couldn't stand the thought of him feeling sorry for her; she was swollen and discolored in the beginning, for a while she had plaster from hip to toe; she looked like shit, and she sounded worse. Those were all good reasons. She probably wouldn't have called him anyway. She knew he had retreated, and that hurt like hell, so she wanted to get past him once and for all. In that sense, the accident helped. The cab company paid all the bills, which was great because there were a lot of them. They gave her six months' leave at work, with pay and an assistant instructed to field all her calls and then fill her in. She would handle what she could handle, most of it through e-mail. She got Bart to relay her phone messages and bring the mail from home, which dwindled down to a trickle of bills and solicitations. And Bart came straight from his job at the auction house every night, first at the hospital, then after two months, at home. From adversity, progress.

ELEVEN

Separate Ways

It was 5 and nearly dark in the city. There had been silence for what – six months now, he guessed. Strong was pleased that he rarely thought of her any more – sometimes over a drink, or on the train. That was good. How was she? He was sure he could call and just be friendly. Maybe he should call. Miranda had been a help. They chatted frequently on the phone. He was pretty comfortable with her.

Strong picked up the phone in his office and started to punch in Natalia's number, then put it down mid-jab. He stared at the instrument for a bit, grabbed his coat and headed for the door. The place was nearly abandoned as he trudged down the hall, and the few people who said "good-night" didn't get a response.

Driving home from the station in the dark, Strong remembered the first time he had seen Natalia at the office,

when she had overwhelmed him. There was no single par-
ticular thing that awed him, but all of them struck him
together – the hair, the eyes, the hips, the legs, the smile,
the attitude, the whole damned package. Strong was sure
he was over her but sometimes, as now, he wondered. He
watched the evening flash by in his headlights and nudged
his memory like a hurtful loose tooth, remembering the
time she had gently pressed her forehead between his
shoulder blades while they waited for the light to change
and he had stopped breathing for a bit. For a moment his
world had changed, as if the floorboards of a familiar room
parted and he tumbled through into a new dimension. He
had forgotten she had had that kind of an effect on him.
And when they had made love, when he was holding on
and she was bucking like a bronco, she had picked him
up and hurled him into a different time and place. He
gripped the steering wheel a little tighter. He was trying to sort out what he truly felt now as he negotiated
the curves homeward through the woods on the blacktop
road. Should he reopen the whole damned thing, or just
let it go? At least it would be exciting.

At home Strong stuck his nose in the bar and emerged
with a glass of wine. What would life be like with her? he
mulled, drifting around the silent house, glass in hand. It
would be exciting, maybe thrilling. His heart skipped a beat.
Damn! He searched for a cigarette but couldn't find one.

Unlike his wife, he never knew what to expect
with Natalia. Consequently, nothing would be taken for

granted. Every moment would be suspenseful. He would be living on the edge. But he wouldn't hold any punches, he told himself, come what may. If it worked, great. If not, tough. He would feel so alive, so on fire. Wasn't that what you were supposed to be – alive? God, maybe this would work. Maybe in some surprising way it would all work out, a second lease on life. Maybe it would be perfect!

Wait a minute. He must be kidding himself. He pushed her to the edge of his mind and went out to stand in the cool night air, poured the wine on the lawn and went to bed. The last thing he thought of was her eyes.

The next day he called her on the phone. Better find out. An assistant answered, which struck him as odd. This was her direct line. When he identified himself, the young man said, "Uh, she's tied up. Perhaps I could have her call you."

"Fuck you, you little shit," is what Strong wanted to say, but instead he said, "That will be fine," and hung up. The rest of the day didn't make much sense. She didn't call, goddamnit. He couldn't believe it.

The next morning, when he got in at 9 he found a hand-written, messenger-delivered envelope waiting on his desk. He flipped it over and read "N. Tsukarova" with her address on the back. Strong dropped it as if it were contaminated, stared at the envelope for a minute, then held it to his nose. She was there inside. He could smell her scent. Still, he didn't open it. Finally, he ripped it open.

"My Ben," it began. He put the letter down. "My Ben." Was he her Ben? Yes, he guessed he probably was, and had been all along. She saw right through him, knew him better than he knew himself. Just one more thing to admire about them, women. When it came to him, they were clairvoyant.

He began a slow orbit of his office relishing the moment, the faintest scent from the letter in hand, moving around his glass-topped desk over to the door, then past the leather couch to the windows with the streets far below, back to the desk. Why had he been playing the court jester, the uncle, the mentor? He wasn't any of those things. He was hers, and some part of him had been from the moment he saw her – her lover, now and forever. What had he been thinking? He longed for her so. He was tempted to put the letter down, get a cab and go over and sit on her front stoop until she came home. He would watch her come down the street, not seeing him, then seeing him, wondering why he was there, walking slowly toward him until she walked right into his arms. If she had been here in his office he would have leapt over the desk, rushed up to her and swallowed her whole. "My Ben ..."

"My Ben,

"It has been so long since we are together. You have experienced so much, too much for any one man or woman. I feel such respect for you, more than any other human being I have known." Was it him, or was her Russian percolating through the English phrases? He laughed, thrilled.

Her written hand was elegant with small flourishes, some Cyrillic carry-over, he imagined. How unique she was!

"I believe you wanted for us to begin anew, after the death of your wife. I, too, wanted renewal, but I felt ill at ease and believe you did too, although we both tried. In any case, it was not the same."

She was right, it was not the same, but that was past now, that was gone, that was over. Why had he waited so long? Were all men so stupid?

"I hope you know that no one can ever replace you for me, not ever."

The sentence ricocheted around in his mind, then tore through his heart and made him take deep breaths.

"I have a new friend now – no, friend is not the right word. You were never my friend, but always something much, much more. I do not have the words. I think this is best, for you and me, although very difficult to write, since you will always mean so much more than I can express, in English or in Russian. If I say good-bye, it is not forever, I feel, since you will always be deep inside me, always in my heart, as I hope – forgive my presumptions – that I am in yours. I remember you, always, and want the best for you. You are such a good, kind, wonderful man, who deserves the best and more.

"Please accept this with all the love with which it is written, and may you have the life you so deserve." Then there was something in Cyrillic, he had no idea what, and it was signed "Natalia"

He sat down dully at his desk and crumpled the expensive paper in his fist. What the hell did that Russian phrase mean? Probably, "So that's it, turkey," or the equivalent. "I love you so much," seemed unlikely, but that's what it was.

"I have a new friend now ..." He felt absolutely ... empty. He remembered coming home after his wife's funeral and standing in the backyard. He had expected to be overcome with grief that awful day, to explode in tears, and to his horror he had felt ... absolutely nothing.

His secretary barged in but saw him sagging at his desk and beat a hasty retreat. Strong didn't emerge from his office until the end of the day.

◆ ◆ ◆

A year passed. Strong was written up in the trades for winning a major new account – TV commercials in the U.S. and Germany for a German carmaker. A U.S. agency doing commercials in Germany was novel. He was thrilled, flattered. His agency had never won something so big – millions of dollars the first year alone. It took them to a new level. He added a team of creative types, plus a few German-speaking executives to keep the client happy. They would come in every morning and the faxes from "the Fatherland", as they began calling it, would be strung out across the floor. Secretly he hoped the news might trigger a congratulatory call from Natalia. One day his phone would ring.

"Hi, it's me. Great going on your new account. *Sprechen Sie Deutsch?*" He was thrilled of course, but kept his feet on the ground. Sweat broke out on his forehead. He sat down.

"*Nein*, no I don't, I had to hire people for that. You're sweet to call. How are you?" He probably shouldn't ask that. Too leading a question. He should just say something to wrap the conversation up, keep it simple and without implication, something like, "We're real busy now. If I had known it would be like this, I never would have pitched the account!"

"I'm fine," she said. "I have missed talking to you."

"You have?" She hadn't said she missed him, just that she missed talking to him. Did that mean something?

"Absolutely. I don't have to explain things to you. You just understand."

"That's true, I do."

"I've missed more than that ..."

He wanted to reach through the wires and cradle her face, kiss her eyes and her lips.

That's the way he imagined it, but of course she never called. After two weeks, he balled that hope up and threw it in the trash. To hell with it. Stay focused. From now on, he would be all business.

When the word got out the agency was hot, potential clients started calling unbidden. Strong couldn't believe his luck, although most of them were just kicking tires and not driving. One, however, caught his attention – a new financial company that only a few years before had been a sleepy, dull utility until its hotshot CEO took over. Now they wanted to conquer the world and had bought up all sorts of companies. They coined the phrase "asset management". Strong was never sure what it meant.

He flew to Phoenix, a city he quickly learned to hate for its incredible heat, for the initial meeting. John Marks Randolph was the CEO's name. The company had its own high rise, with offices as plush as any he had ever seen anywhere. These guys must be doing something right, he thought as he walked into the boardroom with its blond paneling and recessed lighting. There was a modern painting along the wall. Strong didn't dare ask if it was a Pollock but it sure looked like it.

"Benno!" Randolph called out with a glad hand and a big smile when he strode in, followed by three or four aides. No one called him Benno. He didn't think anyone outside his family even knew the name.

"John Randolph, I presume," Strong said, recognizing the man from the cover of *Forbes*. He looked older than the photograph, maybe 50, with wispy blond hair and a high forehead. People called him "the Shark" behind his back.

"John <u>Marks</u> Randolph," the man said. Strong stood corrected.

Randolph wanted a national campaign to put them on the map in the everyday world, preparatory to making their first public offering. Strong realized right off the bat his agency wasn't the one for the job and said so, but Randolph insisted.

"I've seen your stuff," he said. "Besides, I already announced it to the trades." Strong didn't say anything. "You want to know the size of the account?" Randolph asked.

"I don't even know the theme of the campaign," Strong said.

"Ten million. Don't worry about the theme. You'll figure it out. There's a starter check waiting for you on your way out that will show you I'm not kidding." The whole meeting lasted ten minutes. Heading for the elevator, one of the aides drew Strong aside and handed him an envelope. "He's not so bad once you get to know him."

"That's encouraging," Strong said, opening the envelope and looking at the first $1 million check he had ever seen.

◆ ◆ ◆

Strong began a trans-Atlantic commute on Lufthansa once or twice a month, New York to Munich overnight. He chose the German carrier to get in a German mood, listening to the language, eating the food, drinking the wine, even watching a film or two, although he understood almost none of it. It didn't hurt that the young women serving first class seemed pleased to do so, so unlike the

American airlines where everyone acted like he was lucky they gave him a seat and found him a meal.

It turned out Miranda had lived three years in Germany and knew the country well, spoke German flawlessly. He seldom saw her but took to calling her before each trip, which usually required two to three days for business, onto which he would tack at least three days' touring. Why not? He was already there. It was a great way to travel.

"So, you must go to ..." and she would name some place way off the regular tourist track. Strong took notes. She recommended Baden-Baden.

"Why?" he asked.

"Because it is Germany of the past," she had said of the place. "You will see Europe as it was, and better under-stand – and appreciate – what it is today." That set him back. People usually recommended places for the view or the food or the architecture, something in vogue they had read about in *The New York Times* or *Architectural Digest*. She spoke a different language here.

"OK, I'll go."

His most recent meeting in Munich had gone well until Peter, his principal contact and the man who had made the decision to hire the agency, took him to dinner.

"I have a slight problem," the round German said shortly after they were well into their first beer at an inn outside the Bavarian capital. Hunting murals lined the upper walls. Strong was surprised to see several German

Wehrmacht soldiers marching among the hunters. Peter noticed. "Painted in the mid-'30's. Not such a good time," he said.

Strong liked the Germans, couldn't imagine how they had done all that to the Jews, never brought it up of course, but appreciated it when they made sardonic comments about their past. Once Peter had said, commenting on the efficiency of their production line, "We Germans are pretty strict. I guess that didn't sound quite right." Strong laughed despite himself.

He was jealous how easily Peter and his colleagues spoke English, wishing he could lapse into the guttural German sounds which had first seemed so harsh until one night, in a small Nuremberg night spot, he heard a Marlene Dietrich recording of *Ich Habe Ein Koffer In Berlin*, about a woman who had left her heart behind in the German capital. After that, he loved it.

"What problem?" Strong asked, antenna and beer mug raised.

"This is a very German problem. I don't like it, but here it is. With all this unification stuff over the last eight years, and our employment problems, I get a call from the Interior Ministry two weeks ago."

"And they don't like you using an American agency here in Germany."

"Of course they don't like it. Who cares? I knew that when I hired you. German advertising is so bad. But now some of our friends on the right have brought their concerns to the table, as you Americans say."

"What in hell could they want?" Strong asked, draining his mug of the dark beer in hopes of more. "I thought they loved America."

Peter signaled the florid matriarch behind the small corner bar for another beer. "Right, left, who cares? Yes, of course they love America, but not all the time. Ben, it's politics. There are no rules."

Strong remembered why he hated politics.

"Carmakers are vulnerable to the Greens on the left for environmental reasons, and to the conservatives on the right for unions, immigrant and employment matters. We have to be careful. We must walk a narrow line, and still make — and sell — good cars. That is the most important thing. The American market is the key to us, and you are the key to the American market. Don't forget that."

Strong sat up straight in his chair.

"I'm not going to do anything about this problem. I just wanted you to know. Enjoy the dinner," Peter finished. "And watch out for your new friend, Randolph," he said out of the blue.

Strong started to ask how he knew about Randolph, then decided against it. He had a hard time tasting the meal.

◆ ◆ ◆

His meetings over, he drove west across the entire country, which took the better part of the day. The roads were fun, and wonderfully maintained. Peter had arranged one of their top-of-the-line touring cars for him, and he blasted along at 130 with no fear of arrest on the speed-limitless *autobahns*, people fleeing the left lane when they saw his big car looming larger and larger in their rear view mirror. They actually got out of the way, unlike home. What a country!

Miranda's recommendation, Baden-Baden, was a small, neat town that had been a health spa, complete with natural thermal baths, for two thousand years. Strong found a small hotel built around a gravel courtyard, dumped his things and took a stroll. His posture changed to fit the place. He stood more erect, imagining himself a figure from Seurat or Manet complete with black three-quarter coat, top hat and walking stick as he followed the cobbled riverbed that snaked through the town. The air was clear and bright. Flowers lined the riverbanks. He stopped at a café with white cloths on wicker tables, and ate a *sandwich au jambon* in the sun. Why didn't ham sandwiches taste this good at home? Maybe it was the glass of Moselle he had with it.

At the end of the afternoon Strong found himself in front of a Baroque emporium that looked like a cathedral but was a public bath. Mustering courage, he walked in, paid the fare, did his best to follow the German instructions and ended up, stark naked beneath a giant towel, wondering what in hell he had gotten himself into. The attendants, mostly male and unsmiling in their white coats, merely pointed. He shuffled off, feeling very much the ignorant American and praying not to create an international incident by wandering into the women's zone.

To his delight he began to find his way. First came a frigid deluge from a huge shower. Next was a roasting sauna, then another shower, a table with two threatening titans who wordlessly rubbed him raw with tree branches, then hot steam on a marble slab, and finally a high coffered-ceiling pool at body temperature where he floated, nearly unconscious, into bliss. When he heard female voices he realized that the adjacent pool, beneath a cathedral-like dome with Roman statues in the corners, had men and women intermixing casually. Like most Americans, he was not entirely comfortable in the buff, but he loved the open attitude, completely lacking self-consciousness. He wished he had it.

Home, he invited Miranda to lunch. It was his second time to visit her house in Greenwich. "House" was not the right word for a place that took a full minute to drive from iron gate to forecourt. One time, for the fun of it, he had calculated the acreage and tried to project the cost of upkeep, giving up when he lost count of the zeroes.

"You didn't warn me about the mixed doubles at the end," he said euphemistically of the baths at lunch. She laughed.

"I wanted to see your reaction." He thought about that. Later he told her of Peter's warning about Randolph and

German politics. "Not so good," is all she said. He thought about that, too.

He soon became her regular escort. It was an informal arrangement for a formal relationship. He was always correct. She was always impeccable. He had to buy some new clothes. They seldom touched – just an occasional hand on her elbow to guide her here, lead her there – but they looked good together. That seemed to suit her just fine. Him, too. Now that he thought about it, it was perfect. He didn't want a relationship. It would require more than he was willing to give. There were times when you had to be alone. This was one of them. He didn't feel lonely, just removed. Maybe he was getting old.

"Are you enjoying yourself?" she asked him one day as they strolled through her rose garden.

Of course he was enjoying himself. How could he not be? The agency was going great guns, he was thinking of opening a West Coast office, maybe moving the main office to the suburbs and buying a building in New Jersey, Connecticut or Pennsylvania. Natalia was a distant memory, and the thought of his wife only occasionally stabbed him. He had every material advantage, and he suspected, if he stuck around much longer with Miranda, he might have a hell of a lot more. So sure, he was enjoying himself. Why not?

"Yes, I am."

"Good," was all she had said, then took his arm and nestled in. She had never done that before. They walked along.

"I would ask you for dinner but I can't. There are some very boring people I must attend to."

"Of course," he said. For some reason he imagined himself Prince Phillip, walking two feet behind the queen, hands clasped behind his back.

"You can come back later, if you wish."

Ah, there it was. An open invitation, a hook in the water. Come see me later. He should have been thrilled. They walked a bit more in silence.

"But that might not work. Perhaps some other time," she said quickly. He had the feeling that a door had opened and closed very quickly. Why was he so uncomfortable with this whole thing? It all looked good on paper: attractive couple, same age, easy conversation, similar tastes, good manners – all that stuff. That should work, shouldn't it? He should leap into the breach, get it over with, and do the obvious thing: ask her to join him on his next trip to Germany. She would be such an asset, speaking German and all. He suspected the Germans would be impressed with her language and those big emeralds. Next time, he would do it.

He took his leave shortly thereafter.

◆ ◆ ◆

Randolph was not the boor Strong expected. The first test was the check. It didn't bounce. The second was

Strong's outline of the campaign to win broad financial support. Randolph agreed that the obvious – a high-priced television campaign at events like the Superbowl – was too crass. For a man who seemed to be anything but subtle, Randolph was a surprise.

"We don't need a lot of clever, expensive Nike shit," is how Randolph put it. "We're not going after teenagers and their mental equivalents," he said.

They decided that an old-fashioned print campaign in regional and national newspapers like the *Minneapolis Star Tribune* and *The Wall Street Journal* would get them the most for their money, multiple full-page buys with a straight-forward message that people with money to invest would appreciate. Sincerity was the key. Strong added a nice touch: the copy would push them to a web page, where Randolph could change his message daily to fit the economic weather.

Randolph was not a computer person and initially there were no thumbs up. "Let me show you what I mean," Strong said and walked him over to the monitor on his desk. His team had set up a mock web page for Randolph's company. "Here we go," Strong said as he typed in the address and hit "enter".

Strong bounced from page to page, each one a graphic overview of a subsidiary Randolph had bought. It didn't take two minutes before Randolph whooped, "This Internet thing just might be here to stay!" and slapped his knee cowboy-style. "Shit, this is great!" Strong glowed. "Show me how to do it." Strong put him in front of the keyboard, mouse in hand, and before long Randolph was surfing like a veteran. "Hot damn, this is something else!" he said. "I'm going to get me one of these," he said. Strong wasn't sure if he meant a computer or a computer company.

The money from the account flowed in. Strong had a hard time believing it. It was almost too good to be true. The agency took on 15 new people just to handle the media buying, account work and copy. The place was flying.

TWELVE

CLOSE ENCOUNTERS

Natalia felt pretty good about herself as she walked down the street. Why not? She had come through twelve hellish months damned well. She and Bart were playing tennis again, and if she was a little stiff, it was getting better. Amazingly there were no permanent aches, pains or scars. True, she still struggled with her words, especially when she got steamed, but all in all she was fine. Strangers couldn't tell. Friends were patient.

Bart was a puzzlement. She loved him, of course, but not in that way, not the way she had loved Strong. That was just as well. You couldn't go through life on fire. It could consume you. It almost had. Still, she tingled when Strong crossed her mind, which wasn't often any more. When she had learned he was trying to phone her she had immediately written a note to shut him down, turn him off, and turn her off, too. She wasn't going to take the chance of being pitied, coddled, petted and loved all because some stupid taxi had knocked her for a loop. Anyone who wanted her had to take her for what she was, not what she wasn't.

Bart did that. He had been a friend like no other. He restored her faith in her fellow human beings. He valued her honesty, he was kind and sensitive, and he was funny. For too long she had run into people she thought were going to be friends, and then suddenly there would be some miscommunication, some misunderstanding, some indifference that went deep and wasn't incidental but profound, and then she could never be open with them again. Despite her native Russian caution, she had always been anxious to throw open her arms and welcome someone in, without reservation. Early on she had found that often was the end of friendship, not the beginning. With Bart, it was different.

She could see he was working his way through his shadows, groping for the light. He was emerging from a stage and becoming more himself. She suspected that when the process was complete, they would both take another look at themselves and each other. She was wondering what was next when down the street, still far away, she saw Strong and stopped still.

He was in a dark suit and looked good – as always. The hair may have been a bit longer. Was there a new confidence in his walk? There should be, from all she had read in the trades. The man must be rich now, riding high on his new wave of success, clients begging him to take them on, women at his feet. She had seen it before when men got lucky and struck it rich. Early on in her career she had consulted for a regional travel company with a hotshot president who, in the year she knew him, took the firm from regional to national, and then went public and became the number three travel company in the country. The man had changed. He went from being a pretty funny, very smart and relatively considerate guy to a complete shit. She realized that before, his fear of others more powerful had kept him in check, but when he didn't fear anybody, he did what he wanted. He would charm people until they liked him, and then use them mercilessly. "Special friends" he called them, and she supposed they were, since no regular friend would ever take the kind of brute, selfish, mean treatment this guy had put out, all in the name of training employees and improving the bottom line. He would tell outright lies to get people to "compete", pitting them against each other. The whole place had smelled of fear. Some huge consumer product company eventually wooed him away. His company was split up and ceased to exist, exhausted as if he had sucked all the energy out and then left it to die. God, she hated that. She wondered if Strong had this arrogance as she watched him weave down the sidewalk. Should she cross the street and pretend she hadn't see him? On the other hand, it would be interesting to see if she were right.

◆ ◆ ◆

Strong practically ran smack into Natalia. "Jesus Christ," he said, stopping short, face-to-face. It had been more than a year. He had ducked out of the office for a little fresh air, bobbing and weaving through the crowd on Madison Avenue and *blammo*, here she was.

"How are you?" she asked carefully, stepping back and offering her hand. She seemed to be concentrating, looking right at him but not in a friendly way, looking at his face but not in his eyes, as if he were a client. He decided to just mumble something fast and move on.

He couldn't help noticing her ebony hair swept back, held by a ribbon, red of course. Red was always right for her. Her suit's broad shoulders and snug waist showed her figure. The skirt stopped at her knees.

"Fine. Well, you look good," he said, looking off down the block as they shook hands formally.

"You, too."

If he had seen her coming he would have crossed the street. While he was trying to make up his mind what to say next he blurted out, "You have been well, I hope."

That was a lie. He didn't wish her well. He hated easy lies, especially when they came from him. He hadn't used a contraction, just like she used to do. Jesus Christ, this was ridiculous. Make this brief and to the point. Get out of here.

"Just fine," she said, straight in his face.

For the first time he took a close look at her. "You're fine?" She had said it with a sort of challenging air. He suspected what "just fine" meant. She wasn't going to tell him that things hadn't been going so well. "Good," he said with some satisfaction. "Did you see the *Ad Age* story?"

What an egotistical thing to say. Why was he asking questions and prolonging this? He was sorry the minute he asked.

"Yes. I am sure you are very pleased." She almost added, "You jerk."

"Oh, you bet. It's been quite an experience. We're so busy now. If I had known it would be like this, I never would have pitched the account. Fly to Germany at least twice a month. I'm really enjoying this one. And of course, the money doesn't hurt either." He wasn't going to admit that it was a double-edged sword that might, if he didn't play it right, slice the other way and cut him off at the knees if he didn't succeed. He wasn't going to share anything important with her.

He heard his own hollow, stupid cover-up chuckle, put his hands in his pockets and rocked back on his heels. She just stood there. Once, in a dream he had imagined running into her. This was a lot worse.

"I got your letter," he said. He couldn't pretend she hadn't told him to get lost.

"Good." Take that, you cocky son-of-a-bitch.

"Good? Well, I was a little bit shocked I have to admit. I didn't expect it."

"Probably not. I understand."

"You do? No, I don't think so. You see, I had been trying <u>not</u> to call you and then your letter arrived and I ripped it open. I was so glad to hear from you. You remember what the first line said? You probably don't."

"It said, 'My … Ben'."

"Yes, 'My Ben', that's right! Well done! She remembers – remarkable." He did the stupid laugh again. "I read that and then I put it down and thought about it, didn't read any more, you see, I was foolish, so stupid, just … walked around my office thinking 'my Ben' and, truth be told, I was your Ben, that was the funny part. We hadn't talked in so long, I was sure I was over you and then suddenly I wanted to see you right then, wanted to, to – I don't know – hold you, I guess that's what I wanted to do."

He was circling her like a prey in the middle of the crowded sidewalk, looking into her face, spitting the words out. He hated this and loved it at the same time. She had done it to him, and now he was going to do it to her. She had hurt him, and now he was going to hurt her.

"What a fool – I'm not embarrassing you here, am I? Would never want to do that." That shut her up.

"You know what I almost did next? You're not going to believe this: I almost got in a taxi and went over to your place – can you believe that! Sit on the stoop and wait for you to come home. You know what a stoop is, right? Probably don't have them where you come from.

"And then you said you met someone new, someone <u>else</u>, and you weren't going to see me, and I just sat there for the rest of the day, didn't take one fucking call, and I went home and got drunk. That's what I did. You understand what I am saying?"

"Yes, I think so. I'm sorry … Ben, I have to…"

"No, I don't think you do. You have to what?"

"Please …"

"Please, what?"

"Please, no more, Ben."

"No more? No more what? No more of what I feel, no more of what I think, or just no more of me, period? What?"

"Please, stop."

"Stop? No, I don't think so. Well, so you've got a new guy. Great. Everything going fine? Everything <u>OK</u>? I sure hope so." She was starting to cry, he noted. Fine by him. "You know, this is pretty much a one-way conversation here. You might at least try to talk to me. I can promise you it will be the last time."

"Don't. Please stop."

"Don't? Why not? Tell me why not? I asked you a question. I think I deserve an answer." He could be mean when he wanted to, and he wanted to now. "What's the matter, cat got your tongue?"

"Oh … no." The words were all bottled up and wouldn't come out. What would she have said anyhow?

"Hey, don't put yourself out here. I didn't want to run into you either, you know. This just happened. To quote you, 'Sorry!'"

"Me, too. Sorry …" Why had she not crossed the street, let bygones be bygones, gone on with her life, been with Bart? Why had she been so reckless as to take him on?

"Jesus, I've had better conversations with four-year-olds. Don't say, 'Sorry' again. I don't want to hear it."

"I ... won't."

"Good. Goddamnit, that's it? Has it all really come down to this? You know, I really thought we had more. Stupid of me, I know. There never really was anything, was there? Just a little heat and thrill in the night. Easy to let go, eh?"

She wept quietly. "Please ... go."

"Go? Sure. Why not? 'Bye." He looked at her one last time and took off down the street, then came back. "Oh, one more thing. I loved you. I know – 'Sorry'. You don't have to say it. Me, too."

He turned and fled again, livid. He took one last look and saw her with her face in her hands in the same spot he had left her. He gave out a roar of satisfaction at seeing her so wounded. People scattered around him as if he had fired off a gun.

When he got back to his office, he called Miranda and asked her to dinner. She accepted.

◆ ◆ ◆

"Hey, I'm in here!" Bart called out when he heard her come through the door as he bumped around the kitchen of her small apartment. There wasn't a lot of room. Two people were one too many. He was a lousy cook but tonight was going to be special, so he had made the effort:

total take-out.   First, there would be smoked salmon on tiny crackers with capers atop a spot of *crème fraiche* while they chatted on the couch, then over to the small dinner table for vichyssoise, followed by quiche Lorraine with salad vinaigrette, and a strawberry custard torte for dessert in front of the fireplace.   Different wine for each course.   Everything was in its proper little white box with a wire handle in the half-fridge.   It had all cost about $100 for two, plus the wine, which nearly doubled it, but he didn't care.   And he had bought a split of champagne.

Natalia talked differently because of the accident. It had slowed her down, which frustrated her, but she remained essentially the same — sharp, volatile, passionate, full of life.

He, on the other hand, had changed.   He thought differently.   He spent more and more time with her, and less and less time with his other friends. If he had had to describe himself in entomological terms, he would have said he was molting.   Caterpillar to butterfly — something like that.   At work he buckled down instead of treating the office like an interlude between personal amusements.   He could tell people were looking at him as something more than a charming, handsome fixture.   They were beginning to take him seriously.   Perhaps it was because he was beginning to be serious. He was certainly serious about her.   He didn't like it, but there was no denying — she meant the world to him.

"In here!" he reiterated when she didn't reply.   The bedroom door closed quietly, then nothing.   "Hey, are you all right?" he asked coming into the hallway, wiping his hands on his apron. He stood at her door, listening.

"Yes. Yes. OK," she said, muffled. "Out in a minute."

"OK. I've got some treats for you tonight." He headed back to the kitchen with its old-fashioned black and white tiled counter and diminutive gas stove.

"In a minute," she called out.

He was a little disappointed she hadn't noticed the spread on the coffee table in front of the couch. Oh, well.

"OK, here I am," she said, coming through the door a few minutes later. She had changed from her business suit into jeans and a man's dress shirt. He wondered whose shirt it was.

Bart popped the cork on the champagne, poured them both some and offered a glass to her. "For a very pretty lady."

"Something special?'

"Maybe. How was your day?"

"OK."

"OK? That's it? Are they being mean to you at the office? Maybe I should go down there … "

"No. Can't talk."

"What's wrong? You're talking like you did about six months ago."

"Not much."

"OK, then I will do the talking, young lady. Get comfy." They moved into the living room and she nestled into the couch with one leg tucked beneath. She looked beautiful, as always, but sad. He collected himself.

"You know, when I saw you get hit, it felt like the earth stopped." They hadn't talked about this before.

"I agree."

"I bet. No you talking now, just me." She made an "um" noise.

"And you lying there in the hospital, hanging on by a thread, made me take a real good look at myself, think long and hard about who I was, and what I was doing. I was nearly 40 and didn't know. I have grown up more in the past few months than years before that. Couldn't you tell?"

She made another "um" noise.

"So this," he said raising his glass, "is to acknowledge all that, and to say, 'Thank you,' and how much I ... appreciate you. Appreciate is not the right word." This was harder than he thought.

She got up from the couch before he could finish. "You were going to say ... you love me."

"Well, yes, I was going to say something like that."

"You're sweet."

"Sweet, hunh. I'm not sure how you mean that."

"Don't get so ... defen...sive." She worked her way around the word and the couch and stood looking down at the lifeless fireplace. "Bart, I saw him today."

"Oh, shit."

"I agree." Slowly, painfully, she relayed what had happened. It seemed to take forever as she struggled to get the words out.

Finally she finished, "He hurt me."

"That son of a bitch."

"Yes."

"Well, fuck him, if you will excuse the language. We're going to forget all that and just have ourselves one hell of a good night. Sit down and prepare to eat a delicious dinner."

She did, wondering how delicious it would be, knowing full well he could do many things well but cooking wasn't one of them. With each course, he emerged from the kitchen with a new dish and a wink. "I shop well," he said, and they laughed.

He was right. They had a wonderful evening. At the end of it she suddenly got up and said, "I'm going for a walk."

"At this hour?"

"I'll be fine. I just want some time to myself."

"OK." He knew what that meant. He cleaned up while she was gone, then waited alone on the couch. Finally he gave up and went home.

When Natalia came back, he was gone. She loved him, sure, but it was different. She felt bad about that, and bad about Strong, and bad about everything else, as a matter of fact. She lay on her back in bed and let the tears flow down onto the pillow. Wasn't life supposed to get better? It occurred to her that that was a naive American thought, where people thought there actually was a heaven on earth, and that they deserved it. She was Russian. She knew better.

◆ ◆ ◆

Three nights later, Strong got dressed in the house he had come to hate. Walking in the front door now he felt like it was somebody else's home. How could that be? It had been so warm, so welcoming when his wife was there, and now it was an empty shell. How fitting. Everything was in place, but nothing had any substance, depth. The warm human touches had long since disappeared – cut flowers, fruit on the dining room table, garden tended and blooming. His wife had had a green thumb. His was brown, like the grass. Strong was a neat man so there weren't dirty clothes scattered hither and yon, but the place seemed hollow to him, unused. He kept the liquor out on top of the bar now, not bothering to put it away, and made the bed only on weekends. Same with the dishes, which he would rinse but not put in the dishwasher until Saturday or Sunday. He seldom ventured into the living room, never her sitting room, and the den only to watch TV late at night if he couldn't sleep or focus on a book. When he came home he marched into the kitchen to heat something, swung by the bar for a drink, climbed the stairs to get out of his suit, settled down in a chair to read the local paper until dinner was hot, ate and went to bed. That was home for him now. The house felt like it was waiting to be sold.

Strong wanted to look his best for this dinner with Miranda, and had bought a new tie he thought she might like, emerald green with polo players or something, he couldn't quite make out what. He almost wore a suit but realized that would have looked odd in the country, so opted for dark slacks and a camel's hair coat. Not bad, he said to himself in the full-length mirror on the back of the bathroom door. Very distinguished. He remembered having said that to someone before, and it had made her laugh. Very funny.

Miranda looked stunning when she opened the big, heavy door to her home. They had decided to dine *chez elle*, with its huge, splendid kitchen chock full of polished copper pots and pans that aspiring chefs like him would kill for. She was cooking tonight, and so had a long white apron over her creased slacks and cerise silk shirt with rolled sleeves. How can women look so fetching wearing something so mundane, he wondered.

"Hello," she said with a smile and a peck on the cheek, hint of a rare perfume.

"Shit. I forgot the wine!"

"Don't worry. Come in. We'll find something."

They did. He sat at the long country kitchen table sipping as she breezed around stirring pots on the stovetop and peeking into the oven. There were stuffed mushroom canapés and a little paté for *hors d'oeuvres*.

"What's for dinner?" It smelled like lobster.

"Surprise," is all she would say.

Eating delicious *paella*, the conversation ran down to zero. Finally, he put his fork down, looked at the beautiful woman across the table and said, "I can't do this any more."

"No?"

"No. It isn't me."

"Explain," she said, and put down her fork.

"Oh, I don't know. This beautiful house, you, a beautiful woman, somehow I don't fit. All the parts are right except me. I don't make a whole."

She considered him for a moment. He tried to see if he had hurt her, but she was too strong for that. He seemed to be awfully good at hurting people, and he didn't want that, not at all. Looking straight at him she said, "Things don't always work out the way we think they should, the way they 'ought' to. Square peg, round hole."

"Yes." He was feeling very bad, but also relieved. "It's not you," he said, meaning it wasn't her fault.

"No, I didn't think it was. It's someone else. Perhaps that's what's wrong."

"Yes. No. I don't know."

"Do you know what you are going to do?"

"No."

"Call me if you think I can help."

"I don't know how to thank you." He really meant it.

"Have some more wine before you go."

"Thank you. I think I will."

They finished the bottle of wine. She didn't press him. He admired her resilience, truly appreciated it. She must have known this all along. Women were always one step ahead of him. There had been no scene, not even a hint of self-pity or sorrow, although she must have been disappointed.

"Thank you," he said at the door as he was leaving.

She kissed him lightly on the cheek and said, "Don't worry."

He went home, much relieved, still confused.

◆ ◆ ◆

Strong studied the storyboards carefully one last time, packed them up along with the demo tape and headed for the plane. He was going to show Peter personally, with no one else from the agency along in case it didn't go smoothly. He also wanted to sound Peter out about the political problems that might, in the very near future, eliminate the need for any trans-Atlantic commuting whatsoever. The remark about Randolph also had him puzzled.

That was the problem when a small agency won a big new client: the sun rose and set with them, and if you lost the account, you lost not only their business but very likely your entire stable of clients. Two small clients had departed the minute they read he had won the German car account, fearing they would be lost in the shuffle. Others held on but watched him very closely and became more demanding. They would walk at the slightest provocation, he was sure. If the Germans departed, all the others could act like rats leaving the proverbial sinking ship. Randolph and his fast-paced, buy-it-at-any-cost company didn't make Strong feel any better, so instead of feeling confident, secure and good about business, he felt hesitant and doubtful here at his peak. He could never tell anyone that. Certain things you kept to yourself. He almost told Miranda but held back at the last minute. Success wasn't supposed to be like this.

Still fatigued from the little sleep he got in first class, he arrived at Peter's sparely decorated office late the following afternoon, artwork in hand.

"Ben, you look like hell," Peter said when he came through the door.

"Nothing like encouragement from the client," Strong said, and they got right down to work. Strong spread the mechanicals across his desk. Peter mulled them over.

"I almost like them," he said, and Strong's heart took a flip. "No, that is wrong. I almost love them. But there is more of an ... what do they say now ... edge ... I would like to see."

Strong knew right away that he meant a younger audience than Strong had focused on. They spent the rest of the afternoon refining the look the ads would have. The next day Peter took Strong for a tour of the assembly plant, which was surgically clean. Most of the workers wore dazzlingly white smocks. Strong had so many new ideas racing around his mind by the end of the tour that he could hardly sit still. Peter saw it and laughed. He was getting the message.

As Peter drove Strong back to the airport for the flight home, he said, "And forget about that political thing. We have it in hand. Just tighten up the look you are giving us."

Getting out of the car in the airport wind, Strong heard Peter add, "Look, be very careful with Randolph. Guilt by association."

Strong didn't know what to say. "You sure as hell know colloquial English," is all he could think of.

"I went to university there, didn't you know? Cambridge," Peter said and drove off.

Mulling over his comments with a second glass of Liebfraumilch on the flight home, Strong put the Randolph comment aside and focused on this vital client. The Germans were ahead of him, and he had to catch up. It was that simple. Sink or swim.

◆ ◆ ◆

The heads of the departments sat around the table. No one looked glum, but Strong could tell they were worried. They knew he called this kind of meeting only when he had to, preferring one-on-one conferences and talks.

"OK, here's the deal," he opened with. "They" – no one needed an explanation of who "they" were – loved our stuff." A whoop went up, high fives and all that. "Sort of." They all booed.

"No, they really liked it, but think it needs more of an edge. And you know what? I agree with them. Do I have any choice?"

Everyone stopped talking. "Any suggestions? Anyone can talk, there is no right or wrong here, including firing the boss." They laughed a bit. "Just kidding about that." They laughed a little more.

"How about doing everything in sepia?" the receptionist asked timidly.

"Not bad," Strong said, and half-meant it.

"Yeah, we could slip into color at the end," a mousy copywriter chimed in at the far end.

"I could see that," Strong encouraged. "Keep going. You've got the art department worried shitless." Everyone laughed hard at that one.

In the end they came up with about twenty different ideas, most of them completely contradictory. Strong loved it.

"OK, for the next two months you are going to be scarce at home, so warn your spouses now. Anyone wants to sleep here, I'll have cots put in – just kidding. But if you need to call me, here is my cell number." He recited it. "You can call me day or night. Shit, why did I say that?"

The meeting broke up. He could feel the energy. As he was edging out, his office manager approached him.

"Some of this requires training."

The word triggered a pang in Strong. "Just get a different bunch than the last one."

His manager knew about Natalia and Strong, of course, and knew what he meant.

"That girl doesn't do it anymore, anyway. Out of the business, I think."

"She is?" Strong struggled to seem indifferent.

His manager turned into the Men's Room. "Yeah. She got banged up in some accident. Permanent damage, I hear. I thought you knew." The door swung closed. Strong stood there, frozen.

◆ ◆ ◆

"You look a little tired."

He was standing in line at the supermarket with his favorite checker, three kinds of mushrooms on the conveyor belt. He thought he would try to prepare a special omelet tonight. He was about to reply as he glanced surreptitiously at the tabloids, which he always did: allegations about babies from outer space, Michael Jackson being androgynous, another Elvis sighting and several movie stars whom he had never seen before. He must really be ancient. A small sub-hed brought him up short: "'Shark' Swimming in Dangerous Waters?" it said, with a just-recognizable picture of John Marks Randolph. "Add this to the mushrooms," he said, grabbing the paper. Publicity in a supermarket tabloid wasn't good. Too often the absurd things they printed turned out to be true. The checker started to make a wise crack, then saw it was serious and shut her mouth.

In the car he whipped the paper open and found the story. It was some innocuous bit about Randolph scubaing in the Caribbean with a girl half his age. Strong laughed, and then saw a tag that brought him up short. "Of course, the SEC may take a long look at this diver's doings. He may be in too deep when it comes to tallying profits." What in hell did that mean?

◆ ◆ ◆

At home that night he lit a fire and opened a fresh bottle of red wine. He had asked the checker for a cigarette – she gave him two. He was determined to do something sinful, and this was it. The wine was rich and good, and the cigarette went well with it, although it made him slightly dizzy.

He guessed he should apologize to Natalia. He had said some very vicious things, verbally stabbed her over and over, and now he had found out she had been defenseless. It was like hitting a quadriplegic – completely unfair, out of all cosmic order, just mean and awful. Every time he thought about it he felt sick. And how badly had she been hurt? Was it permanent? Could she lead a normal life, have children, get back to her old, feisty self? He couldn't imagine her any other way.

So what should he do – call, write, visit – what? He had to do something to expunge his soul. He imagined a call, stumbling over his words, unable to see her reactions, awkward pauses on the other end. That wouldn't work. A letter would be heartless, cowardly, the easy way out. No, he would have to do this in person. Shit. Maybe there was another way. Maybe she had forgotten the whole thing. After all, she had her other guy. Sure.

And what did he want, what did he expect? He took a puff and a sip, the smoke swirling up through the light toward the ceiling. He guessed he wanted to repair the slashes and gashes, heal the wounds, bind her up, make her whole and send her on her way. No hard feelings, he was sorry for what he had said. He wished her free and happy. Him, too. That's what he would do.

THIRTEEN

GOING DOWN

The car campaign was coming together. Strong worked long, long hours week after week, sometimes staying overnight in the city, having missed the last train out. Peter called him countless times, but he refused to even hint what they were creating.

"Wait, just wait. You won't be disappointed," he had said each time. He wished he were sure of that. In his mind he wanted it to be meaningful, not just gorgeous. He wanted to say something that people would understand, not just present a car. He kept telling his people, "It has to have a bass line," meaning there had to be more than eye candy and commercialism. Finally he figured it out: it's not the destination, it's the drive. No words but those at the end. Just the sounds of driving the car for 25 seconds, starting, turning, cruising, braking, in rain, in snow, on gravel, on the highway.

Meanwhile Randolph was missing in action. Strong had placed four calls to him and hadn't gotten a single response. Something was up when a client didn't return your calls, you could be sure of that. Question was, what? The guy had paid a bundle of money already, Strong had sent him the final copy and Internet graphics for his campaign, he had three more executives on board to hand-hold and supervise and create. They were chomping at the bit, Strong could tell, proud of what they had done and anxious to see it launched. Strong felt the same way but couldn't let on.

He held a team meeting to boost morale. Everyone crowded into his office instead of the boardroom. It had a more intimate feeling.

"Ben," the young woman who was running the show said, "we're having a hard time fine-tuning this campaign. We need to get more of a feel for this client."

"I know what you mean, although they keep paying us on time," Strong said.

"Thank God for that," the young creative director said with a guffaw. Strong knew what it was like to be a young creative director. Until one of your campaigns took off and your name got known on the street, you were expendable. The guy was glad to have a job. Strong knew.

"Look, I have an idea," he said. "Why don't you two fly out to Minneapolis to their Midwest office and run by the copy you have now. Demo the web page. Get a sense of what they like and don't like. I can't get any response from these people now. I think their heads are elsewhere. Don't make a big deal of it, just sort of do it informally. Tell them we want to test some of our ideas without showing the boss. They'll understand."

"I talked to those folks when I was doing the research," the woman said. "They might go for it. Anyway, I've never been to Minneapolis."

"Well, from what I hear, everyone is white," the creative guy said. "I am not going to find any homeys there."

"Don't give me that homey Puerto Rican pride stuff," Strong said. "You're about as much a homey as I am, unless gang garb has changed to button-downed shirts with a bow tie."

"Hey, have to look out for the brothers."

"No, that's what the black guys say. For you, it's *mi barrio*. Get out of here."

They left the next day. Strong waited for their call. When it came it was not what he expected. "Ben," the woman said, "there's something up and we can't figure out what it is, but no one will look us in the eye." Oh, shit.

"Fly back. We'll talk about it," he said. Looking out his office window, the city seemed cold, distant and lonely. He suspected it had something to do with that phone call. When he finally got Randolph on the phone two weeks later, he pressed.

"John, what's up?" He explained the reluctance to work with his people in Minneapolis.

"Nothing, Ben. A little SEC thing, not to worry."

"Not to worry? I am worried. We are about to launch a major information campaign and give you a big presence on the web. Your credibility is on the line." He didn't add that it was his credibility, too.

"You let me worry about my credibility, fella," Randolph said. "Just do your fucking job," he said.

"John, we need a check to cover these media buys. They are too big for our pocketbook." Strong had lined up a big buy in *USA Today*, *The Wall Street Journal*, *The New York Times* and *The Washington Post* plus regional papers all over the country. They all had the copy and were ready to go, waiting for cold, hard cash or the agency's guarantee – either would do. Strong's controller had been talking with his counterpart at Randolph's company all week. A wire transfer was imminent. More than $2 million was on the line.

"The fucking check is on its way. When have we not paid? Jesus Christ, I can't believe you are talking to me about money! We have been paying you through the goddamn nose!"

He had Strong there. They had been. "Yes, yes, believe me, I appreciate that."

"So stop talking to me about money. I don't want to ever have this conversation again. Are you listening to me?"

"John, we need to cover these buys."

"Then cover them," Randolph said, and hung up.

Strong was worried. Blunt clients were supposedly a sign of "open communication," but he never believed it. If they were pissed, they were pissed, and you better look

out. Now Randolph was stonewalling him. With a financial client, if they lied, then you lied, and who knew where
that could lead? SEC didn't stand for Sweet Easy-Going
Compadres. They collected heads. Prison was a distinct possibility with those guys when they got rolling. It had never
happened in the ad world, but what prosecutor wouldn't be
delighted to set a precedent and get his name in the papers?
A friend of his in the brokerage business knew some of the
SEC types, and he said they were young and vicious. They
never smiled. Strong was scared. Jesus Christ.

On the other hand, he had a responsibility to his client.
Randolph had been paying them good money, and it was a
good campaign. Strong had never seen another quite like
it – an attempt to establish a presence in financial circles
by going directly to the public. Strong liked the plebeian
approach. Everyone else schmoozed the financial types
and courted *The Wall Street Journal*. Randolph was a renegade. So was Strong. OK, Randolph was a jerk, too, but
you didn't dump clients because they were assholes. If that
were the case, you could write off half your clients, and
probably a lot more. The check would arrive. He had to
make the buy. Stand by your man, as the song went.

"Go with it," he told his media people. "We'll cover it."
It wasn't everyday he made a phone call that exposed him
for $2 million-plus.

The next day they were all over the newspapers.
Randolph left him a voice mail message: "Hey, guy, great
show. Our phones are ringing. It's a pleasure to have Wall

Street kiss a little Phoenix ass!" Strong guessed that was good news, but there was still no check. He had his controller call at the end of the day. Nothing.

A day later they tried again with no result, just promises. His controller came in and closed the door. "Ben, this is going to get serious very fast. We have a payroll to meet next week. We can do it, but when the media demand payment for those buys, we are going to be shit out of luck! In two weeks, the guillotine drops."

Three days later his attorney called. "Ben, can we have lunch?"

"Tom, the last time we had lunch it was to tell me some very bad news. I couldn't eat a thing, and I had to pay for the meal. Forget lunch. What's on your mind?"

"Ben, I heard some nasty shit on the street about your client, and I wanted to give you a heads-up." Strong didn't need to ask which client he was talking about.

"Keep going," Strong said, and the attorney did.

◆ ◆ ◆

In the hallways at the end of the day, the place was quiet, very quiet. Clearly, word had gotten out. The sleek computers, the blond European furniture, subtle wool carpet, original 19th century posters on the walls that he had with the help of his wife collected over the years, all seemed to mock him now. He began looking at them as expenses, not assets. As each hour of the day had passed with no word from Randolph, Strong fought harder to ignore the obvious truth: he had been snookered plain and simple. Randolph had burned him for more than two million. He wouldn't need to read *The Wall Street Journal* stories about the investigation by the SEC, creditors screaming for blood and Congressional action, and the inevitable retreat into bankruptcy. He knew in the pit of his stomach it was all coming as sure as winter followed fall, and in the course of a surprisingly few weeks, it did. He might never get paid – in fact, that was almost certain. So then the question was, what did he sell to raise cash, whom did he let go and how did he stay afloat? The ship was going down.

"Creative accounting"is what they came to call it euphemistically in the press. Strong later heard it straight from Randolph's mouth when he staggered into Strong's office the day after his Senate testimony, where he had been, for a bright business executive, surprisingly forgetful.

"Ben, old boy," he had started off, swaying a bit in the doorway. Strong's assistant hand-signaled that maybe she should call Security. Strong waved her off.

"You want some coffee?" he asked. Randolph laughed and pulled a flask from his jacket.

"You want some bourbon?" he asked and took a swig. "Well, Benno kid, the jig is up, as they say. I'm cooked, medium-rare. Federal vacation's just around the corner. Thought you might sympathize." He collapsed onto the couch, oddly festive. It couldn't be just the booze. Strong would have been slashing his wrists. He couldn't find it in himself to be genuinely angry, although sitting across the room from him was the man who had just stolen several million dollars and probably killed his agency. Where was his outrage?

"So let me tell you what happened," Randolph, clearly not caring if Strong listened or not. Strong happened to be in the room.

It had all started early on when Randolph and his flunkies over-extended themselves with a bad purchase – a New Mexico water-drilling outfit that used new "environmentally friendly" technology.

"It was our third big deal," the man said. "It looked awfully good on paper. We had all sorts of contracts lined up with the Interior Department. A sure thing. Six million in the first six months of business without doubt." He took another swig from his pocket flask.

The technology had been novel. Unfortunately, it didn't work well in bad weather, and it had been one of the worst winters in the Southwest in 50 years. They didn't find water when the contracts required. Bye-bye Interior Department. So Randolph and the boys had hedged their financial report – nothing completely illegal – but postponed reporting the failure by six months. That gave them time to complete two more buys that looked good, so when the bad news came it was drowned out in the din about their new purchases.

"News people are incredibly stupid," Randolph said with laugh.

That had been their first error, a relatively small one from which they could have recovered had they not done it again, but of course they did, and covering up became just another business strategy they used whenever it was convenient. It became increasingly convenient, until late reporting was nothing compared to their other subterfuges. In the end, their assets didn't even come close to their liabilities. The trick had been to never put them side by side on the same piece of paper. "Same as the U.S. government," Randolph said.

Strong wondered how long this dissertation was going to go on. He didn't particularly want to hear the details of one man's compact with the devil.

"You're getting bored," Randolph said out of the blue. "So fuck you. I'm going to jail. Wife's already split. Shit." He slouched back in the couch, small, defeated. Strong almost felt sorry for him.

"What about our media buy?" he asked, knowing the answer.

"Sorry 'bout that," Randolph said. "You were our last chance. Almost worked, too. Took in a lot of money, thanks to you. Almost kept the wolf away from the door. Almost. Shit."

"And it didn't matter who you took down with you, right?" Strong didn't like to sound moral, but he couldn't let the son of a bitch off the hook that easily.

"Don't look so forlorn. You got lots of company."

"How nice. Fuck you," Strong said. He crossed the room in two strides and snatched the man off the couch. Randolph struggled to his feet and tried to free himself. "Out, you prick." Strong pushed him to the door and marched him out of the office. "Keep walking," he said as he propelled Randolph down the hallway. A few heads poked out the offices registered shock as the duo marched by.

When they got to the reception area, Strong said, "Don't let this bastard back in here unless he is waving a check. No, make that cold cash," and that was the last they saw of John Marks Randolph. He got five years federal "vacation".

By then Strong's premonition had come to pass. Over-the-transom business stopped immediately after the SEC story first broke in the *Journal*. Then there were fewer and fewer assignments from the existing clients, always with good reason. It took a month before Strong realized how quiet the place had become. For the hell of it one afternoon he pretended to read a magazine in the reception area. The phone rang exactly twice in twenty minutes.

Some of the key people in the agency took longer and longer lunch hours. Strong knew what that meant: job-hunting, interviewing. Inside, he also felt quiet, diminished, imploding, getting smaller by the day. Commutes home on the train lasted a lifetime each night. Rain streaked the rushing windows.

◆ ◆ ◆

n the fall Shelley and her husband – Strong could never remember his name – came for a weekend visit. The guy had taken a post teaching computers or something at a small college in Massachusetts. He looked the part – shock of uncontrollable sandy brown hair, glasses and a pale complexion that could stand about thirty solar seconds before turning pink. At least he was earning an income. Strong wondered how long his own would last.

He was determined not to do anything to offend the guy during their stay, although he had no idea how he should treat someone who wore a pocket protector on Saturday and Sunday. Shelley didn't seem to mind.

The first night they had cooked lobster. Shelley patiently showed her husband – Henry – how to crack the claws and pry out the meat. He proved quite adept at it after a few misfires, including one that launched his fork halfway across the dining room. By the end of the night they were all spattered with lobster, butter and beer, of which they had drunk a considerable amount. Strong heard himself say "inauspicious" with an extra "sh" in there somewhere, and hoped no one else heard it. Shelley suppressed a giggle. Henry said, "Ah, a new word. I believe I have made up a few myself this evening," and they all exploded. Strong started to like the guy. He noted that Henry took a great deal from Shelley but then indicated, very clearly, when enough was enough. All right! he said in his mind. Shelley could be a real pain.

The next day they were all a little fuzzy. Shelley and Henry took off for a hike upstate. Strong had a Bloody Mary after they left, then took a nap. When they returned at 5 he was preparing the grill for a large steak. "Does Henry eat meat?" he asked his daughter when they were alone.

"Henry eats anything," she said with mild disgust, probably a result of her brief but unsuccessful attempt to be a vegetarian at college.

"Hitler was a vegetarian," Strong had said over Thanksgiving dinner her sophomore year, slicing into the moist bird his wife had spent hours fretting over in the kitchen. Shelley had given him a very narrow look, but that was her last Thanksgiving with no turkey.

Cooking over the outside grill in the Indian summer evening, he sipped wine, poking haphazardly at the thick slab of meat. Shelley had come out with a glass of her own dressed in sweats, which Strong refrained from admonishing her about. At least she wasn't pierced. "They'll learn," he imagined his wife saying about changing fashions, if that's what the recent baggy sartorial vogue could be called. Strong doubted it. He was secretly delighted Shelley had started to add a touch of make-up now and then. It brought out her natural beauty, the almond-shaped eyes and bowed lips. For the longest time she had gone without, coupled with a "take-me-as-I-am-or-not-at-all attitude. Age forged some realizations on its own. He sipped his red wine, mellow.

"I'm pregnant."

Strong nearly dropped his glass, spilling some wine on the brick patio. Shelley jumped deftly back. "What?"

"You heard me."

He was completely uncertain of what to say next. He felt immediately old, which he realized was totally selfish. "Congratulations."

"Men never get it," Shelley said without any blame in her voice.

"Oh, God, I'm going to get a lecture," Strong said.

"When I told him, Henry said, 'Really? No kidding,' like I just got an A on a test or something. I could have slugged him, but then he sort of giggled. The next day he admitted he didn't feel very fatherly."

"I know just what he means," Strong said. "When your mother told me about you, I had no idea what to say or think. It didn't really make any sense at all until you actually came along."

"And …"

"Surprisingly, it all fell in place. I loved you unreasonably, unconditionally, instantly. Felt very protective, the veritable lion in the jungle sheltering his young, although now I understand they occasionally devour their pups." He took a sip of wine.

"Cubs. What a disgusting idea."

"I never considered that," Strong continued, "although murder crossed my mind once or twice."

"I'll bet. Like the time I snuck out my window when I was 14 … ."

"You were 13, and yes, then, and the time you called me an old goat. Actually, I think you said 'old shit'. You thought it was the 'shit' part I got mad at. Actually, it was the 'old' part."

"Dad, you are something else."

"Yup. That's a good way to put it." He gave her a kiss on the forehead, which made her smile.

She took the big fork and poked at the meat.

"An old family tradition, meat-poking," he said.

She imagined some hairy humanoid in a darkened cave standing over a fire and poking away, a distant relative who had started an enduring family tradition millenia ago. Good ol' Uncle Charlie, 200 times removed. She shook her head. "Weird. I do the same thing at home. Runs in the family, I guess."

"Your mother would have agreed," he said.

"You still miss her, don't you?" Shelley said.

He sipped some more wine, didn't say anything and was glad it was dark on the patio. "I do, too. Sometimes a lot."

"Don't start on that now. I won't make it through dinner," he said.

She tucked her head into his chest, gave one brief sniff, and then shook it off. They both stayed silent for some time, then Shelley added, "Hey, you're not dead, you know."

"What?"

"You're not dead."

"I think I have heard this somewhere before, and from you, in fact. Of course I'm not dead. What are you saying?"

"Don't put yourself out to pasture just because you're going to be a grandfather."

"That makes me feel so conflicted I absolutely have no idea what to say."

She laughed. "I love you, Dad. You don't seem like a grandfather, but then I don't seem like a mother, either."

"Time marches on."

"Well, get in step then."

He began marching in place, waving the poking fork like a baton and leading an invisible band. "Yes, ma'am. Will do." A salute. He had absolutely no idea where he should be going.

"Oh, be quiet. I'm hungry."

Henry bounced in. "Ooh, steak. Hey, this is a <u>great</u> weekend."

"Hi, dad," Strong said.

Henry groaned. "Oh, no. You told him!"

"Of course I told him."

"Ben, I have absolutely no idea what I am doing," Henry confessed. "Shelley seems to know, so do you. Am I the only one?"

"Nope," Strong said. "Don't worry. You'll figure it out." Sage advice. He hoped it applied to him.

When they left the next afternoon for the drive home, it had turned cold. Winter was coming on. Strong was sorry to see them go.

◆ ◆ ◆

His office manager was waiting for him in his office when he got in an hour late that Monday morning.

"Hi," Strong said as he went to his desk. "What's up?"

"I was thinking it might be a good idea to sub-lease some of the offices down at the end of the hall," the man said with a bright air.

"You know, why don't we lease out some of offices down the hall?" Strong reiterated with a twinkle in his eye.

"Now why didn't I think of that?" his manager asked, affecting his gayest mannerism, the limp wrist. Strong laughed.

"So, how bad is it?" the man asked, trying to remain light.

"Not good," Strong said. "Do you really want to know?"

"I guess I do. Maybe I can help somehow."

"That's a very kind thing to say," Strong said, meaning it. "Well, we are down to four clients, and I am waiting for a call from the Germans. Dreading a call, actually."

"If that comes, let's close up shop and throw one hell of a party," the man said. "Go out with a blast."

"I like you better and better," Strong said.

◆ ◆ ◆

The trades had it all over their front pages for a week that his agency was on the ropes. Then the story faded to the inside and finally disappeared altogether. Natalia read every one. When the story disappeared, she made discreet inquiries among friends in the business. Nip and tuck, was all she could discover. No one knew much. She felt sorry for him. Like Icarus, he had flown too close to the sun. Her youthful surmises about life had proved all too accurate: it wasn't a benevolent universe; it was sneaky and mean. Get one step ahead and it nailed you just when you raised your glass to celebrate. That made her really sad.

Bart could see the pain she was in, and knew what brought it on. He wished he didn't, but he did. Maybe it would pass. That's all he could hope for. He began distancing himself from her as best he could. He started by not calling her every day, then stopping by only twice a week. He spent more and more time at the auction house, working late most nights, often the last one to leave. The night security guard got to know him by name. Finally he skipped five days completely. That hurt, but the part that really hurt was that she didn't say anything about it.

◆ ◆ ◆

She wanted him, she wanted him, and she wanted him – Ben – from the first cup of coffee in the morning to the last glass of wine at night. Walking down the street, moving around the apartment, lying in bed at night, anywhere, anytime, she wanted him. It was that simple.

Natalia went over their last angry encounter a hundred times in her mind. She saw him coming down the sidewalk, said hello, and watched him slowly explode in front of her. She had expected arrogance, almost wanted it to prove how human and weak and frail he was, how undesirable and unworthy and awful, and instead he was angry and frustrated and hurt. She had hurt him badly with her note. He tried to cover it but it all bubbled up out of nowhere and then he had attacked and left her in tatters. Who could blame him?

Now he was wounded anew. First she had done it, and now his business. Piling on, they called it in American football. Life had piled on, and he was seriously damaged. What should she do?

She knew what she wanted to do. It was obvious. She wanted to go to him and wrap her arms around him and hold him so close and tight she would come out the other side. But she couldn't just walk up and say, "Hi!" She didn't want him to feel sorry for her because of her stupid speech problem, she didn't want him to feel apologetic because of their last encounter, nor hold on to her like a straw for a drowning man. She wanted them both to be whole and complete and together forever and ever and ever. That's what she wanted. Now they were both damaged goods. That actually made her laugh. Outside, snow began to fall. Christmas, the best time of the year, was coming.

◆ ◆ ◆

"Do lunch?" she asked cryptically when he picked up the phone.

"Well, well," he replied, "a voice from the distant past."

"Yes. Do lunch?"

"I guess I owe you an apology." He was sitting at his desk with not much to do.

"We can talk about it. Some water over the dam."

"Hell of a lot of water. Pretty big dam."

"Yes, well, maybe. May I take you to lunch?"

"You must have been reading the trades."

"I have been. My turn to say, 'Sorry.' Come to lunch."

He thought for a moment. He didn't want to go, but he had decided long ago that he should apologize in person and make sure she was whole. He guessed this was it. "OK," he said finally.

"Good. I want you to meet somebody. May I bring Bart?"

"Bart. That's your guy, right? Sure, love to meet him," he said as evenly as possible. "Where?"

"Tomorrow, 1 PM, Rainbow Room Grill, it's my treat. See you there," she said and hung up. Strong looked at the phone for quite a while trying to figure out what he was thinking.

◆ ◆ ◆

The minute she saw him alone at the table she knew how badly he was hurt. He looked drawn, gray, haggard, older, practically a different man. He saw her and rose from his chair. She put on a happy face, unsure of what to do next.

When he had looked up, Strong had been struck by how beautiful Natalia was. She wore a beige suit with a shortish skirt, matching blouse, and high black-and-tan heels. She seemed very tall, demure and smoldering at the same time. Her hair was held back by a dark red scarf and there was some jewelry, but he was so dazzled he couldn't really see any of it. She was late by 15 minutes. A piano player played Cole Porter and Irving Berlin, absurdly romantic for that time of day. Strong was sure that most of the people there were couples like them, escaping a business day for a lunch that was anything but business.

They shook hands. He didn't see anyone with her. "You look well," she said over her shoulder as he held her chair and she sat down. "Bart will be late. He got held up at the office."

"Fine. Looking forward to meeting him. You look beautiful, as always."

"Thank you. May I have a drink?"

"Of course." He signaled the waiter, who took her order and left.

"Well ..." she said pointlessly.

He came right to the point. "I heard about the acci-dent a few weeks ago. I'm so sorry. Are you OK now? Does everything ... work?"

"Well, I wasn't for a while, but now I'm fine. I had to relearn how to talk, if you can believe that. I am much better with contractions as a result." They both laughed, and she told him the whole story. He was aghast.

"And Bart was with you through all of this? I've got to meet this guy. Good for him."

"Yes. You can see why I feel about him the way I do."

"Yes, of course. This is a whole different picture. To you two," he said, raising his glass in time to the piano music. "When is he coming? I want to thank this man."

"He should be here any minute. Anyway, that's my life. Tell me about yours."

He did — about John Marks Randolph, and the Germans, Shelley pregnant, and Miranda of course. He didn't go into details about Miranda. They ordered lunch, salads both, and another glass of wine.

"You've been busy," she said.

"Yes, I have. I guess we both have." He added a laugh, not knowing what to say next. She was wondering herself.

Lunch arrived with no Bart in sight. Strong waited for her to pick up her fork, then picked up his but stopped. "Shouldn't we wait for him?" Natalia shook her head no. He plowed ahead.

"How do I say this? I feel so ... bad ... awful ... about what I said to you on the street that day. There is just no excuse. I've never wanted to undo something so much in my life. I would ask you to forgive me, but I can't imagine that you could."

"Yes, that hurt." She wasn't going to let him off the hook right away. Did he really mean it? Yes, she guessed he did. After a bit she said, "Forgiven," and touched the back of his hand. A shock raced up his arm and into his chest.

"Thank you. God, this is good," he said of his food. He was suddenly starved. "Can I come to the wedding?" he asked out of nowhere. She hadn't said anything about a wedding, but he could tell.

"Absolutely. I'll send you an invitation."

"Swell. When is it?"

"We are considering a couple of dates, but haven't decided yet. Probably in June."

"Perfect," he said, eating more. Boy, he was hungry. She seemed to have lost her appetite and just poked at her food. "Worried about Bart?"

"No, I'm sure something came up. Usually he calls, but not always."

"Sure." He took another bite. "Tell me how you met." Natalia took a breath and relived the night she and Bart had met at the SoHo gallery. She described him, how handsome he was, how funny, how kind. Strong listened and for some reason felt sad.

"You must love him very much," he said, taking a sip. She had stopped eating.

"He is a special person."

"Well, here's to you both," he repeated, lifting his glass. "To your happiness." He drank, then ordered another.

"Thank you," she said, pushing the lettuce around with her fork. She didn't seem to be enjoying the meal much.

They made small talk, but later he could never have said what it was about. At the end, when they were both standing and ready to leave, he touched her face and gave her a brief buss on the cheek. "Take care," he said. Her skin was soft, incredibly soft, and smooth.

<u>Take care?</u> she thought. <u>Take care of whom, of what?</u> The only thing she wanted to take care of was him.

She waited for him to say more but he didn't. There was nothing to do but head for the elevator. Just before she got there she turned and asked, "Ben, would you do me a favor?"

"Of course. Anything. Just ask."

"Let's dance," she said. She might as well have hit him with a left hook again.

"Dance? Don't you remember? I'm terrible!" He wasn't going to dance with her. This was the end of lunch, the end of the affair, and he wasn't going to prolong it.

"Oh, come on. Just this once. Practice for the wedding." She came up close to him but he backed off.

"Can't. I really can't. Got to get back …" No, no, no.

"To the office," she finished for him. She had used that excuse a thousand times herself. "I know. Well … goodbye, Ben."

"'Bye," he said.

She entered the elevator, the doors closed, and she never looked back.

Natalia stood alone in the wood-paneled elevator car, going down, down, down 65 long and lonely floors. She glanced up at the descending floor numbers. What else was there to do? It may have been Christmas, but she didn't feel like it – Christmas, her favorite time, when people smiled more on the city streets – at least she did. Christmas, with all the images of home, snow in the forest, people bundled up, presents the night before, Grandfather with his huge pipe and nicotined moustache making her laugh, Father Frost himself. It didn't seem like Christmas now.

Well, that was that. Who had said that you can't go back? Whoever it was, they were right. Time to move forward. Grow up, she told herself. You have become too American, expecting it all to work out in the end. Remember you are Russian at heart, and always will be.

The elevator slowed halfway down, her ears popped, and the doors opened. People got in. She did her best to disappear in the back. The doors closed and they resumed the plunge. Another thirty seconds and they bobbed to a halt at the lobby, the doors opening once again and everyone rushing out except her. She could see men and women, dressed in long black overcoats against the cold, march to and fro. A small group gathered at the door to the elevator, waiting for her to exit so they could pile in. She gathered herself and plunged back into the real world of cheery holiday music and the vague scent of evergreen. Outside stood the huge tree, already deep in shade thanks to the enormous buildings. Where should she go from here? What should she do? She had absolutely no idea. The music changed – Bing Crosby singing *White Christmas*. Oh, no, not that song. Tears welled up behind her eyes.

"Do you really want to dance?" a voice said behind her. "Are you sure?"

She staggered to a stop, unbelieving. "How did you …"?

"Express elevator." Strong said.

She looked around at the hundreds of marching people. "Dance … here?"

"Anywhere. Just be sure you want to."

"I want to. This is crazy."

"Yes, I suppose it is. Let's dance."

"OK," she said, trying not to envision the stir this was going to cause in the middle of the huge, bustling lobby. They must both be crazy.

He pulled her into the middle of the aisle between the two ranks of elevators. She had the distinct impression that everyone in the entire world was staring. "Just like the ones we used to know …" the music went.

He began carefully and apart, very correct and ramrod straight. People saw them and altered course with curious glances. They formed an eddy in the flow of humanity. He stood a head above her, not moving, so she placed her left hand on the small of his back and put her right hand in his left, and began.

The moment they began to move, people stopped and gawked.

The music was simple and slow, which made Strong relax a bit. Out of the corner of his eye he noticed that the men in the crowd looked doubtful, but the women were smiling.

Strong got the rhythm with her help and began enjoying himself. People moved back a little, making a small circle. He heard a giggle of appreciation or two, which helped his confidence. Natalia followed perfectly – or was she leading? He couldn't tell. He kept his hand light on her back to be sure he was being correct, proper, completely neutral as they danced through the lobby. He sensed she moved a little closer, but maybe not. He could smell her perfume, strong and sweet with just a trace of her body beneath. He was amazed: she seemed to glide effortlessly with every step. It was like dancing with a cloud. They didn't speak. Her hair brushed his cheek. Whatever he did, wherever he went, she was right there, and closer, he thought, now definitely closer. He felt her chest brush lightly against his, and then the firm swell of her stomach, and occasionally her thighs. He felt like they were on air. The gathered crowd, now growing, gave way when they neared, like something alive and responsive. She smiled at his amazement that this was so good, so delightful, so natural. She made it easy, like so many things, like making love. He looked down at her, thinking he should say something, and didn't know what to say. Goddamnit, his heart was in his mouth. He could hear a sort of low thrum, as if the news of their dance was rippling through the lobby and people were beginning to talk. She looked at him, her head tilted quizzically as if waiting to hear, holding back, reserved.

"He's not coming, is he?" he asked.

"No, he's not."

"And you're not getting married, are you?"

"No, I'm not."

"So why did you tell me you were?"

"Because I didn't want you to think I was just sitting around waiting for you."

"Were you?"

"Yes."

He kept moving with the music for a few more steps as it dwindled down to nothing – "And may all your Christmases be white …" – then stopped. She bumped into him with her eyes closed. She kept her head down but there were tears leaking down her cheeks, he saw. He reached his arm further around her back and slowly pulled her all the way in. She melted against him. The crowd, led by the women, burst into applause. He had forgotten they were there.

"I'm not sure I can talk," he whispered in her ear.

"Not necessary," she replied into his shoulder. Oh, man, he thought. Oh, man. There was a spark that ran from his heart smack into her chest and held them there. He was looking in her eyes and thought he might fall in. Finally he recovered, gathered her up and fled outside, the murmur of amazement and appreciation following them out the door. He even heard one guy say, "All right!"

"I have missed you so much," she said as they stood looking up at the tree as the lights came on.

"Me, too. I am tired of acting like your uncle, which I am not, although God knows I'm old …"

She put her finger to his lips before he could get the rest out.

"Help me now – where do we go from here?" he continued.

"You mean, your place or mine?"

"No. Well, yes. But beyond that."

"I don't know, but let's get going," she said. And they did.

FOURTEEN

GOING HOME

She walked into her apartment without turning on the lights, but he could hear the rustle of clothes as she shed her suit jacket in the hall and continued with the skirt in the bedroom with the drapes drawn until she was on the bed and down to practically nothing.

He was having trouble with his breathing again, and with his clothes. He could see her tanned skin beneath some very white, skimpy lingerie, lying on her back with one leg up, sort of shielding herself from him. When he pushed it aside, it flew open like it was spring-loaded and she was pressing against him like there was no tomorrow. She was always ahead of him in bed and here she was once again already wet as rain and trembling and shivering and he was still trying to get undressed.

She couldn't wait. She exploded for the first time even before he put his hand between her legs, and when he did she grabbed his wrist with both hands and held him inside until there was more rain. By the time he was stripped he stood out like a bazooka which she grabbed and then buried everywhere she could until he didn't know which end was up. Finally there was no going on and he just let go and she absolutely shrieked in delight tinged with what sounded like pain to him and then exploded in tears.

Jesus Christ, he thought, how do I match that?

A little later, after they had lain on the bed with the sweat cooling off and fingers wandering, she said, "That was something else." Her face was still damp.

"Boy, I'll say," was all he could think to reply.

"God, thank you so much," she said.

"You never have to ..." he started to say and she hit him with a pillow and they both laughed. He put his hand in the right spot and she said, "Oh," and it started all over again. "Oh, oh." God, this <u>was</u> something else.

Later Strong said, "I was thinking about you the other night," up on one elbow looking down at her and smoothing her chest with its dark little nipples.

"And what did you think?"

She lay back, comfortable, satisfied, relaxed on her bed with him beside her. She was glad they were together again. If it had been illicit love before, now it was just love. This was a good man. She rolled over and put her head on his chest.

"Can we start something new?" she asked.

"Oh my God ..."

"No, no, not like that. I wanted to ask, do you miss her? Can I ask you that? Am I allowed?"

He didn't say anything for a minute, working his way through his thoughts. When he had sorted them out, he said, "I do and I don't. Deep down I do, but closer up you've pretty much blotted everything out." He wondered if he should feel good or bad about that. He also wondered if that would upset Natalia. She could be so touchy.

"That's OK. I think that's nice, actually. And now I can tell you I love you," she said simply, putting her head down on his chest again. They lay, comfortable together, for a while. She realized she had wanted to say that for a very long time.

◆ ◆ ◆

They went everywhere together. After all, Strong was free to be with her now. She began phoning him regularly at the office. His secretary caught on and put her calls right through.

He wanted to meet Barton. Natalia had told him all about Bart. They met and it was all fun. Strong liked Bart immediately, especially when Bart said practically at the git-go, "Don't worry, she hasn't told me everything, thank God."

Before long they were playing tennis together, taking turns running Bart into the ground. Natalia seemed to glow in the reflection of the two men. Strong was surprised how young he felt. He actually liked seeing them, Bart and her, together.

Besides tennis there were art galleries and small French restaurants. Strong found he was looking forward to each encounter with them. New York seemed to transform itself into a friendlier, more intimate place with distinct neighborhoods and unique shops, restaurateurs with faces and smiles, fountains and parks. It seemed they were always together. He felt like *Jules et Jim*, and couldn't for the life of him imagine Bart as gay. At the end of the evening there was sometimes an awkward moment when they were all trying to decide who was taking her home.

One day, at Bart's insistence, they went sailing out on Long Island, his family's place, and what a place it was. It took them two minutes to get down the drive. There were manicured lawns and gardens, trellises and bright flowers, a pool or two and "the summer house", a rambling affair that could have housed three families easily and was clearly something from the late 19th Century, when money came in waves to some who then built grand homes. Bart's mother was nice, greeting them at the door with the same easy manner her son had, white hair and beautiful skin with understated jewelry and a great smile. She clearly loved Bart and was probably delighted he hadn't showed up with another male "friend".

They had lunch out on the terrace overlooking the Sound and their small inlet, with Bart's 36-foot sailer rocking easily at the dock. Strong kept looking at the contrast between the young woman and the older, admiring them both, to his own surprise. He admired Natalia for her passion and beauty. She still made him want to lean over and slide his hand up her skirt. He had done so once in a restaurant when no one was looking and she had just watched him steadily with a small smile on her face, opening her legs slowly, her eyes closing when he touched home.

But now the older woman was holding her own. She had come to terms with life and age and was comfortable with them both. Her skin was wrinkled, but not her spirit. In fact she was downright youthful, with sparks in her eyes and a wonderful sense of humor. He felt privileged to spend just this short time with her. She bantered with all of them, flirted with him, treated Natalia like a worthy opponent and her son like a beloved pet. Bart was having fun, even doting. Strong could see why. At the end of lunch Bart's mother rose regally, sent them to the boat and disappeared, to take a nap, Bart later explained. They trooped down to the boat and got underway.

From Bart's angle, it was enjoyable and awkward at the same time. This was the home he had grown up in, and bringing them here was like letting them take a peek at his insides. It was him all over, from the obvious privilege of the place to the graciousness of his sweet, sweet mother, to the boat nodding in the water, and all that that implied.

He only hoped he could emulate his mother's grace and charm however old he got. There was an age limit for gays these days, it seemed. He was in the clear, but everyone he met, gay or straight, had that look of, "How long are you with us, my friend?" which really pissed him off. He didn't think of himself as *gay* gay. He wasn't even sure he was gay at all, maybe just neutral. This house, this boat, this beautiful setting was part of him but it wasn't all of him, and he only brought people here whom he knew would recognize there was more to him than bucks and "breeding", as some of his mother's more pretentious friends said.

Bart was particularly anxious what Natalia would think, she with the sleek, sleek body and piercing eye and wit and enormous determination. Her return to speech had been a lesson for him in sheer, raw will power.

As soon as they had cast off she had gone below and emerged in a high-cut, tightly wrapped one-piece suit in cerise that covered up everything and revealed it at the same time, thin and snug as it was. She wore it with nonchalance, of course, her body brimming out of it at all the right places, the muscles of her taut, flat stomach undulating beneath the thin fabric. Bart thought she might be capable of writing him off as some privileged stereotype in her post-Marxist philosophy (she may have gotten out of Russia but some of Russia must have come with her) so he was watching her carefully for hidden scorn. All through lunch she said little, her attention riveted on his mother. His mother *was* riveting, he had to admit, but he was surprised and delighted that this young, vibrant woman whom he had come to love had quickly gotten beyond her inhibitions (if she had any – he wasn't sure) and turned to his mother like an oasis in the desert. More and more he took note of Natalia's physical beauty, her olive skin, the high cheekbones, the impenetrable eyes, the brushed, wild raven hair, always a dash of red on the mouth or the chest or the hair – somewhere. And she didn't ever wear a bra, not since he met her. He thought of that more in terms of courage than lust. He always liked it a lot. Things might have been different for him if there had been more women like her around when he was growing up.

As for Natalia, this was paradise. She had grown up in a country filled with drab colors, broken concrete and damn few smiles, and this was the Garden of Eden. Didn't they see that? Such beauty, such honesty, such gentility. What else could heaven be? It couldn't last. Well, maybe not, but she was going to enjoy it while it did. Once she would have hated people like this, convinced it was wealth that allowed them to be what they were, but now she saw the world from a different perspective. She wondered if she had been seduced by good fortune and all its accoutrements. She didn't think so, because it wasn't the things she loved, it was the people. She thought they could have had as delightful a lunch in a cramped apartment in the Bronx as this elegant acreage on Long Island. Bart's mother certainly seemed bigger than her setting. And nothing could replace these two men, not for her. This *was* heaven. She almost pinched herself.

The boat moved easily through the water. The big gray-shingled house began to blend into the coast around it, the rocks and lapping sea. She turned her face into the wind to let it blow her hair back, her eyes almost shut now. It was cool, the light starting to fade, with shafts of sun shooting through clouds from the horizon, emulating some absurdly romantic 17th Century painting of the harbor of Venice.

Strong leaned back against the gunwale, his hands clasped behind his head, eyes closed by the fading sun. A wind came up. He was enjoying himself with these two more and more. He realized had been given a rare chance, to live two happy lives. One life had come, he had been completely happy, and then another had begun, this one so different, and he was happy again.

How beautiful she is, this girl, Strong thought. How exquisite. They were beginning to have simple fun together. He was actually pleased that the passion was wearing off so he could relax, take a breath, sit back and enjoy things with her, simple things like grocery shopping or reading the Sunday paper or taking a walk in the park at the end of the day. It was different than before, with his wife. He was more protective, sheltering, proud of Natalia, like a parent. He loved her. It was awfully good.

Strong turned his head to see the clouds to the east, evening coming on with a darkening sky and a slight chill. He liked Bart, liked him a lot, was happy to see him at the helm, trimming the sails, running the show, the captain of this ship. They looked good, these two together, both dark, tan, muscled, and young.

No one talked. They all seemed to know when not to. How rare, even among friends, Strong thought. He felt special about them, felt like he could take everything he had inside and give it to them, hand them his thoughts, his secrets and even his fears, down to the soles of his feet, everything, and they would take it all happily. He knew she would. He had learned some things, by God, and now he was learning more. He would give it all to them. She already had most of it.

With no warning, a gust came out of the east and pushed the boat hard over. Bart easily swung the helm into the wind so the boat came back even, and asked Strong to help trim the sail. The sky was dark all of a sudden. Strong wondered if he should be concerned. Bart looked at him and said, "Just take the sail half-way down," then glanced toward land and the house. They weren't there. A curtain of rain not 200 yards distant had cut them off, but Strong knew where they were and where they should be going.

As for Natalia, she was a little anxious, looking at the storm. These Americans had no real understanding that things could change in a second, that life could turn on a dime. She loved them, she loved living here, but they were naïve. Life for them was a straight line from here to there with no revolutions, no hatreds, no fears, no people who came in the night with long knives to settle past debts. Theirs was not a vengeful God. Hers was. Americans were so simple: They thought reason would always prevail. Forgotten fears began to seep into her.

"We're fine," Bart said. Strong wished he believed him. Another gust came up, and with it, driving rain. It suddenly felt cold. In seconds they were drenched.

"There's rain gear below," Bart said evenly, looking over his shoulder at the weather and not at them, "but we should be home in a few minutes, so I wouldn't bother. Go up forward and trim that sail," he said to Strong with no tone in his voice at all.

Strong wasn't on his feet two seconds when he heard Bart say, "Look out!" and another gust shoved the boat hard over. Natalia started to fall. Strong grabbed the back of her suit to keep her from hitting the deck as her feet went out from under her. She was so beautiful, so powerful, and at the same time so frail and exposed in this suddenly violent storm. It was good to feel her in his grasp, to help her, protect her, cradle her fall, save her and watch her bounce once on her bottom. She looked so surprised that Strong started to laugh. Natalia came up off the deck to give him a piece of her mind when another gust heeled the boat hard over and she went right over the side. Bart stared unbelievingly.

Without a moment's thought Strong dove into the water. He could see her a few feet down, thrashing and flailing as he swam to her. She seemed not to know he was there at all. He looked at her, waved to get her attention, but to no avail. Suddenly he realized she was in a panic and mustn't be able to swim. Over his shoulder, through the water, he saw the boat begin to turn. Bart was heading back for them.

With a quick, sharp blow he hit Natalia full on the jaw. Payback, he thought of their meeting a long time ago and laughed out loud, swallowing water. She went immediately slack and he grabbed her beneath the arms and around the chest. He was running out of air so he clawed his way back to the surface with her heavy load in his arms. When he bobbed up, the boat was just coming around. Bart hurled a life preserver their way with one hand while lowering the mainsail with the other and holding the tiller with one foot. Strong caught the preserver and held on as the boat maintained speed in the blasting wind. Bart lashed down the helm and pulled the line hand-over-hand until he grabbed Strong and then Natalia. She was coming around, thank God. The two men hauled her on board like a flopping fish. This is all going to make a great story when we get back, he thought. In fact, they all laughed about it once they tied up. Bart's mother had come down to the dock trying not to look worried. She gave them a glass of port to warm up, and clucked about how stupid they were while petting her son on the head with great pride. It took Natalia two days to shake off her fears.

◆ ◆ ◆

L ater that summer they went to Europe together – Strong, Natalia and Bart. It was an odd arrangement, one they could never explain to other American tourists. After a while, they stopped trying. They had a wonderful time.

When they returned he and Natalia went to his house in the country, but it wasn't right. Neighbors, old friends and memories haunted the place. It was another life. One day he said, "Let's go some place else," and she had agreed. He knew it would be difficult for Shelley – and it was – but he had no choice. He sold the house.

Strong felt older. Not old, or weak or tired, just older. It was as if he had stood up straight to see a little farther and discovered he couldn't see very far at all. Time was, he could see the future, or thought he could. Now it was no longer clear to him. It was open, blank like a sheet of paper.

Strong sold the agency. Peter and the Germans had kept it afloat, then slowly the recalcitrant clients began to return, but he no longer had the stomach for it, even though the car campaign had been a huge success. He made a pretty good bundle on the sale but not enough to do whatever they wanted, whatever the whim. There was no private plane. They rented a house in the Pennsylvania farmland not too far from Philadelphia.

One night, reading, Natalia looked up from her book and said, "I miss Bart." Strong was shocked. He had been thinking exactly the same thing. They got on the phone immediately. Bart sounded wonderful. He came that weekend.

Gradually he came more and more. When they bought an old colonial farmhouse a few months later, one reason was that they knew Bart would love it. It was small with warped pine plank floors and rough beam ceilings from the time of George Washington. There was a room upstairs for Bart, opposite their small bedroom, and another guest room off the kitchen below. The living room covered half the first floor and had a huge fireplace which kept them overheated in winter. It was what they wanted.

Natalia and Strong never married. They decided they didn't want to. Living in sin shooed away people they didn't like, and brought closer the ones they did. Bart eventually took up residence, doing his art auction business on the Internet when he wasn't traveling to Madrid or Paris. When the boy was born, Bart was there to help, the little creature screaming day and night for the first two months until he finally decided to join the human race in a civilized fashion. He was dark, like his mother, and younger than Shelley's little boy. They called him Boris, after her father. They had a good, happy life together.

After a few years, Strong changed noticeably, he saw in the mirror. He looked old, his face was thin and angular, and he had a hard time keeping up with Boris, who learned to be gentle with him at his mother's direction. He would put out his small arms to his father who pulled him into his lap and read. That was their favorite pastime. From *Cat in the Hat* they moved up to *Tom Sawyer* pretty fast. Time was racing.

Natalia hardly aged at all, but Strong was moving fast. He was leaving her behind. It was all right. The end of life was like the beginning, you changed quickly. Boris grew taller by nearly a foot. He was in kindergarten. Strong felt awkward when he first took his son to school. All the teachers assumed he was Boris's grandfather. It caused them some embarrassment, which he dispersed with the comment, "I know what you mean. That's exactly what I feel like sometimes!"

Shelley and Henry got to be regulars. They would come for a weekend with their son, Ben, named after his granddad. It was funny having a son and a grandson the same age. The boys didn't mind. They treated each other like brothers, good and bad. Bart and Henry were an odd combination, but seemed to like each other because they would never associate with someone remotely like the other were it not for this crazy familial amalgam. Of all of them, he suspected Shelley would one day be the core.

He could see Bart growing to love Natalia more and more, never saying anything about it, always his friend, but loving her more and more. And he saw she looked at Bart sometimes in a special way, too. Well, that was right. That was good. He couldn't keep up with her anymore, and didn't try. He had to let go. It was a matter of seasons.

One December, late in the afternoon, snow underfoot and the trees bare, Strong was walking the woods when he stumbled on a branch and started to catch himself when he felt a tear inside, a rip. It felt like his heart. How appropriate, he thought on his way down, oddly removed and objective, I'm falling down like some old man. I wonder what's next?

He hit the leaves on the frozen ground and rolled over, everything in slow motion and beginning to flicker, like the movies. He lay there, watching the sky. He thought he should be cold, but he wasn't. He didn't think he could move, though.

And then his wife came and sat beside him. Strong was shocked and sat up. "Jesus, you scared the hell out of me!" he said.

"Sorry," she said.

"You look great," he said. She did, too. "Where the hell have you been? You look awfully good."

"You look tired," she said.

"Thanks a lot. I've been busy."

"I can imagine."

"Now don't give me a hard time. At least I didn't do anything stupid." He wanted to tell her everything she had missed, but he wasn't sure how much she already knew.

"I didn't think you did. Don't be so defensive."

"Actually, I've been having a hell of a good time," he said.

She laughed.

"You know, it's been interesting, I mean the whole thing. I was slow at first but once I got going, I started to learn pretty fast, really learn some things, by God. Love can be different, that's for sure." He was excited. At last they were talking again, picking up the conversation that had been interrupted so long ago. He had wanted that.

"How do you mean?"

"I loved you, and then I loved Natalia, but they were different kinds of love. Does that make sense?"

"Sure," she said.

"You think I'm bull-shitting you."

"Not at all."

"Well, you left me awfully damned fast there. That wasn't easy."

"Hey, I wasn't exactly running the show."

"Sorry," he said.

"OK."

"Well, you look great. No leaving me now, OK? This is all new to me. I need help."

"OK."

He looked around and to his surprise they were all sitting down to dinner together – his wife and Natalia next to Boris and Bart and his mother, and Shelley and Henry with Ben II, here in the woods of all places. Even Miranda was there, thoroughly enjoying herself and looking very fine. What was this? There was white linen and silver and wonderful food with red wine and they were all laughing dressed in white like the snow, and Bart was with Natalia and they were together and that was fine, that was the way it should be, the way he had hoped it would be, tanned and muscled and young and together. How funny! Dinner *al fresco* in the woods in the middle of winter, and it wasn't even cold, Strong noticed, nor warm – just pleasant, really pleasant.

His wife sat next to him at the head of the table and took his hand and he felt wonderful, alive and jubilant and free and happy, really happy as he rarely had been ever before, and perhaps never had. It was so good to see her again, so good to have them all together, together for the first time really, his whole life here before him to see. Bart stood and made a toast and everyone rose and raised their glasses, and damned if Strong didn't start to cry.

Looking at them standing together he realized that the parts of his life all fit. Each part needed the other to be whole. He needed one kind of love to appreciate the other. He guessed it was that way with other things, and that there were no half-truths, no incomplete sentences. Some just took longer to finish. There was no success without failure, no up without down, black without white, good without bad. There really was nothing to fear. He saw that now. Why had it taken him so long? He had suspected so from the beginning. It was wonderful to find out it was true. What a life!

His wife took his hand. They rose from the table together without saying anything. The others smiled at them and continued on. Bart was telling a funny story now, and they were all laughing. Shelley and Boris looked up and she said, "'Bye, Dad."

It was time to go. He glanced at his wife who smiled at him, without pity. She had been waiting for him to under-stand. Now he did. It was worth it, he said to himself. It was all worth it. God, what a life! It filled him with joy.

They turned slowly into the stars, hidden beyond the sun.

◆ ◆ ◆

B art and Natalia found him a few hours later, worried when he didn't come home. He was laying peacefully on his back, looking lifeless at the stars, a small smile on his face. Evening had come on, and it was cold, but his hand was still warm.

◆ ◆ ◆